INSPECTOR FRENCH AND THE BOX OFFICE MURDERS

The suicide of a sales clerk at the box office of a London cinema leaves another girl in fear for her life. Persuaded to seek help from Scotland Yard, Miss Darke confides in Inspector Joseph French about a gambling scam by a mysterious trio of crooks, adding that she believes her friend was murdered. When she fails to turn up the next day, and the police later find her body, French's inquiries reveal that similar girls have also been murdered, all linked by their jobs and by a sinister stranger with a purple scar . . .

SPECIAL MESSAGE TO READERS

INSPECTOR FRENCH AND THE

BOX OFFICE MURDERS

FREEMAN WILLS CROFTS

LARGE
PRINT

First published in Great Britain 1929
by
Wm Collins Sons & Co. Ltd

First Isis Edition
published 2018
by arrangement with
HarperCollins*Publishers*

A catalogue record for this book is available
from the British Library.

ISBN 978–1–78541–618–7 (hb)
ISBN 978–1–78541–624–8 (pb)

Published by
F. A. Thorpe (Publishing)
Anstey, Leicestershire

Set by Words & Graphics Ltd.
Anstey, Leicestershire
Printed and bound in Great Britain by
T. J. International Ltd., Padstow, Cornwall

This book is printed on acid-free paper

Contents

CHAPTER
ONE

The Purple Sickle

Inspector Joseph French, of the Criminal Investigation Department of New Scotland Yard, sat writing in his room in the great building on Victoria Embankment. Before him on his desk lay sheet after sheet of memorandum paper covered with his small, neat writing, and his pen travelled so steadily over the paper that an observer might have imagined that he had given up the detection of crime and taken to journalism.

He was on a commonplace job, making a *précis* of the life history of an extremely commonplace burglar. But though he didn't know it, fate, weighty with the issues of life and death, was even then knocking at his door.

Its summons was prosaic enough, a ring on the telephone. As he picked up the receiver he little thought that that simple action was to be his introduction to a drama of terrible and dastardly crime, indeed one of the most terrible and dastardly crimes with which he had ever had to do.

"That Inspector French?" he heard. "Arrowsmith speaking — Arrowsmith of Lincoln's Inn."

A criminal lawyer with a large practice, Mr Arrowsmith was well known in the courts. He and French were on friendly terms, having had tussles over the fate of many an evil-doer.

"Yes, Mr Arrowsmith. I'm French."

"I've a young lady here," Arrowsmith went on, "who has just pitched me a yarn which should interest you. She has got into the clutches of a scoundrel who's clearly up to no good. I don't know what he's after, but it looks mighty like a scheme of systematic theft. I thought you might like to lay a trap and take him redhanded."

"Nothing would please me better," French returned promptly. "Shall I go across to your office?"

"No, it's not necessary. I'll send the girl to the Yard. Thurza Darke is her name. She'll be with you in half an hour."

"Splendid! I'll see her directly she comes. And many thanks for your hint."

Though he spoke cordially, French was not impressed by the message. Communications purporting to disclose clues to crimes were received by the Yard every day. As a matter of principle all were investigated, but not one in a hundred led to anything. When, therefore, about half an hour later Miss Darke was announced, French greeted her courteously, but without enthusiasm.

She was a pretty blonde of about five-and-twenty, with a good manner and something of a presence. Well but plainly dressed in some light summery material, she looked what she evidently was, an ordinary, pleasant, healthy young woman of the lower middle classes. French put her down as a typist or shopgirl or perhaps

2

a bookkeeper in some small establishment. In one point only did she seem abnormal. She was evidently acutely nervous. There was panic in her eyes, tiny drops of perspiration stood on her face, and the hand in which she grasped her vanity bag trembled visibly.

"Good morning, Miss Darke," said French, rising as she entered and pulling forward a chair. "Won't you sit down?" He gave her a keen glance and went on: "Now, if you'll excuse me for two or three minutes I'll be quite at your service."

He busied himself again with his papers. If her nervousness were due to her surroundings she must be allowed time to pull herself together.

"Ready at last," he went on with his pleasant smile. "Just take your time and tell me your trouble in your own way and it'll be a strange thing if between us all we'll not be able to help you out."

The girl looked at him gratefully and with some surprise. Evidently she had expected a different kind of reception. French noted the glance with satisfaction. To gain the confidence of those with whom he had to deal was his invariable aim, not only because he valued pleasant and friendly relations for their own sake, but because he felt that in such an atmosphere he was likely to get more valuable details than if his informant was frightened or distrustful.

"So you know Mr Arrowsmith?" he prompted, as she seemed to have a difficulty in starting. "A good sort, isn't he?"

"He seems so indeed, Mr French," she answered with a suggestion of Lancashire in her accent. "But I really can't say that I know him. I met him this morning for the first time."

"How was that? Did you go to consult him?"

"Not exactly: that is, it was through Miss Cox, Miss Jennie Cox, his typist. She is my special friend at the boarding house we live at. She told him about me without asking my leave. He said he would hear my story and then she came back to the boarding house and persuaded me to go and tell it to him."

"She thought you were in some difficulty and wanted to do you a good turn?"

"It was more than that, Mr French. She knew all about my difficulty, for I had told her. But she believed I was in danger and thought somebody should be told about it."

"In danger? In danger of what?"

The girl shivered.

"Of my life, Mr French," she said in a low tone.

French looked at her more keenly. In spite of this surprising reply there was nothing melodramatic in her manner. But he now saw that her emotion was more than mere nervousness. She was in point of fact in a state of acute terror. Whatever this danger might be, it was clear that she was fully convinced of its reality and imminence.

"But what are you afraid may happen to you?" he persisted.

Again she shivered. "I may be murdered," she declared and her voice dropped to a whisper.

"Oh, come now, my dear young lady, people are not murdered in an offhand way like that! Surely you are mistaken? Tell me all about it." His voice was kind, though slightly testy.

She made an obvious effort for composure.

"It was Eileen Tucker. She was my best friend. They said she committed suicide. But she didn't, Mr French! I'm certain she never did. She was murdered! As sure as we're here, she was murdered! And I may be too!" In spite of her evident efforts for self-control, the girl's voice got shrill and she began jerking about in her chair.

"There now," French said soothingly. "Pull yourself together. You're quite safe here at all events. Now don't be in a hurry or we'll get mixed up. Take your own time and tell me everything from the beginning. Start with yourself. Your name is Thurza Darke. Very good now; where do you live?" He took out his notebook and prepared to write.

His quiet, methodical manner steadied the girl and she answered more calmly.

"At 17 Orlando Street, Clapham. It's a boarding house kept by a Mrs Peters."

"You're not a Londoner?"

"No; I come from Birkenhead. But my parents are dead and I have been on my own for years."

"Quite. You are in some job?"

"I'm in charge of one of the box offices at the Milan Cinema in Oxford Street."

"I see. And your friend, Miss Jennie Cox, who also lives at Mrs Peter's boarding house, is typist to Mr Arrowsmith. I think I've got that straight. Now you mentioned another young lady — at least I presume she

5

was a young lady — a Miss Eileen Tucker. Who was she?"

"She was in one of the box offices at the Hammersmith Cinema."

"Same kind of job as your own?"

"Yes. I met her at an evening class in arithmetic that we were both attending and we made friends. We were both bad at figures and we found it came against us at our work."

French nodded. The name, Eileen Tucker, touched a chord of memory, though he could not remember where he had heard it. He picked up his desk telephone.

"Bring me any papers we have relative to the suicide of a girl called Eileen Tucker."

In a few moments a file was before him. A glance through it brought the case back to him. It was summarised in a cutting from the Mid-Country Gazette of the 10th January of that year. It read:

"TRAGIC DEATH OF A YOUNG GIRL.

"Dr J. S. Jordan, deputy coroner for South Eastern Surrey, held an inquest at the Crown Inn, Caterham, yesterday morning, on the body of a young girl which was found in a quarry hole about a mile from the town and not far from the road to Redhill. The discovery was made by a labourer named Thomas Binks, who was taking a short cut across the country to his work. Binks reported the affair to the police and Sergeant Knowles immediately visited the scene and had the body conveyed to the town. The remains were those of a girl of about twenty-five, and were clothed in a brown cloth coat with fur at the collar and cuffs, a brown skirt and jumper and beige shoes and stockings. A brown felt hat lay in the water a few feet away and in the right hand was clasped a vanity bag, containing a cigarette case and holder, some loose coins and a letter. This last was practically illegible from the water, but enough could be made out to show that it was from a man of undecipherable name, breaking off an illicit relation as he was going to be married. Dr Adam Moody, Caterham, in giving evidence stated that death had occurred from drowning, that there were no marks of violence, and that the body had probably been in the water for two or three days. At first the identity of the deceased was a mystery, but Sergeant Knowles handled the affair with his usual skill and eventually discovered that she was a Miss Eileen Tucker, an employee in the box office of the Hammersmith Cinema in London. She seemed to have been alone in the world, having lived in a boarding house and no relatives being discoverable.

After considering the evidence, the jury, with Mr John Wells as foreman, brought in a verdict of suicide while of unsound mind."

"A sad case," said French sympathetically when he had finished the paragraph. "I see that the jury brought in a verdict of suicide, but you think the poor young lady was murdered? Now, just tell me why you think so."

"I know it! I'm sure of it! She wasn't the kind of girl to commit suicide."

"That may be, but you've surely something more definite to go on than that?"

"No proof, but I'm as certain of it as if I had been there. But what she told me about the man shows it wasn't what they said."

"I don't quite follow you. What did she tell you?"

"She was in trouble through some man, but not the kind of trouble the letter said. There was no love affair or anything of that kind. It was money."

"Money?"

"Yes. I thought at first she had got into debt to this man and couldn't pay and I offered to lend her what I could; it wasn't very much. But she said it wouldn't help her; that the man had her in his power and that she was frightened. I begged her to tell me particulars, but she wouldn't. But she was frightened all right."

"I don't want to suggest anything bad about the poor young lady, but doesn't it look as if he had found her out in something that she shouldn't have done? Tampering with the cinema cash, for example?"

Miss Darke looked distressed.

"That was what I feared," she admitted, "but of course I didn't let her know I suspected it. And of course I don't know that it was that."

French was frankly puzzled.

"Well, but if all that's true, it surely supplies a motive for suicide?"

"It might have with another girl, but not with her. Besides there was the letter."

"Yes, you mentioned the letter before. Now how does the letter prove that it wasn't suicide?"

Miss Darke paused before replying and when at last she spoke it was with less conviction.

"I looked at it like this," she said. "From the letter it would be understood that some man had got her into trouble and then deserted her. From what she told me that wasn't so, and from what I know of her it wasn't so. But if that's right there couldn't have been any letter — not any real letter, I mean. I took it the letter had been written by the murderer and left in her bag to make it look like suicide."

In spite of himself French was interested. This was a subtle point for a girl of the apparent mentality of this Miss Darke to evolve from her own unaided consciousness. Not, he felt, that there was anything in it. The probabilities were that the unfortunate Eileen Tucker had been deceived and deserted by the usual callous ruffian. Naturally she would not tell her friend. On the other hand he considered that Miss Darke was surprisingly correct in her appreciation of the psychological side of the affair. The older French grew, the more weight he gave to the argument that X hadn't performed a certain action because he "wasn't the sort of person to do it"; with due reservation of course and granted an adequate knowledge of X's character.

"That's a very ingenious idea, Miss Darke," he said. "But it's only speculation. You don't really know that it is true."

"Only from what she said," returned the girl. "But I believed her."

"Now, Miss Darke," French said gravely, "I have a serious question to ask you. If you knew all these material facts, why did you not come forward and give evidence at the inquest?"

The girl hung her head.

"I know I should have," she admitted sadly, "but I just didn't. I did not hear of Eileen's death till I saw it in the paper the day after and it didn't say where the inquest would be. I ought to have gone to Caterham and asked but I just didn't. No one asked me any questions and — well, it seemed easier just to say nothing. It couldn't have helped Eileen any."

"It might have helped the police to capture her murderer, if she was murdered," French returned. "And it might have saved you from your present difficulties. You were very wrong there, Miss Darke; very wrong indeed."

"I see that now, Mr French," she repeated.

"Well," said French, "that's not what you called to talk about. Go on with your story. What can you tell me about the man? Did Miss Tucker mention his name or describe him?"

Miss Darke looked up eagerly, while the expression of fear on her features became more pronounced.

"No, but she said there was something horrible about him that just terrified her. She hated the sight of him."

"But she didn't describe him?"

"No, except that he had a scar on his wrist like a purple sickle. 'A purple sickle' were her exact words."

"H'm. That's not much to go on. But never mind. Tell me now your own story. Try to put the events in the order in which they happened. And don't be in a hurry. We've all the day before us."

Thurza Darke paused, presumably to collect her thoughts, then went on:

"The first thing, I think, was my meeting Gwen Lestrange in the train."

"What? Still another girl? I shall be getting mixed among so many. First there is yourself, then Miss Jennie Cox, Mr Arrowsmith's typist, then poor Miss Eileen Tucker, who died so sadly at Caterham. And now here's another. Who is Gwen Lestrange?"

"I met her first in the train," Miss Darke repeated. "I go to my work most days by the Bakerloo tube from the Elephant to Oxford Circus. One day a strange girl sitting beside me dropped a book on to my knee and we began to talk. She said that she came by that train every day. A couple of days later I met her again and we had another talk. This happened two or three times and then we began to look out for each other and got rather friends. She was a very pleasant girl; always smiling."

"Did you find out her job?"

"Yes, she said she was a barmaid in the Bijou Theatre in Coventry Street."

"Describe her as well as you can."

"She was a big girl, tall and broad and strong looking. Sort of athletic in her movements. She had a

11

square face, if you know what I mean; a big jaw, determined looking."

"What about her colouring?"

"She was like myself, fair with blue eyes and a fair complexion."

"Her age?"

"About thirty, I should think."

French noted the particulars.

"Well, you made friends with this Miss Lestrange. Yes?"

"The thing that struck me most about her was that she seemed so well off. She was always well dressed, had a big fur coat and expensive gloves and shoes. And once when I lunched with her we went to Fuller's and had a real slap-up lunch that must have cost her as much as I could spend in lunches in a week. And she didn't seem the type that would be getting it from men.

"I said that I couldn't return such hospitality as that and she laughed and asked me what I was getting at the Milan. Then she said it was more than she got, but that there were ways of adding to one's salary. When I asked her how, she smiled at first, but afterwards she told me."

French's quiet, sympathetic manner had evidently had it's effect. Miss Darke had lost a good deal of her terror and her story was coming much more spontaneously. French encouraged her with the obvious question.

"She said she had got let in on a good thing through a friend. It was a scheme for gambling on the tables at Monte Carlo."

"At Monte Carlo?"

"Yes. It was run by a syndicate. They had a man there who did the actual play. They sent him out the money and he sent back the winnings. You could either choose your number or colour or you could leave it to him to do the best he could for you. If you won you got your winnings less five per cent for expenses; if you lost of course you lost everything. But the man did very well as a rule. He worked on a system and in the long run you made money."

In spite of himself French became more interested. The story, he felt, was old — as old as humanity. But the setting was new. This Monte Carlo idea was ingenious, though it could only take in the ignorant. Evidently it was for this class that the syndicate catered.

"And that was how Miss Lestrange had made her money?"

"Yes." Apparently Miss Darke had not questioned the fact. "She said that as a rule she made a couple of pounds a week out of it. I said she was lucky and that I wished that I had an obliging friend who would let me into something of the kind. She didn't answer for a while and then she said that she didn't see why I shouldn't get in if I wanted to. If I liked she would speak to her friend about it.

"I wasn't very keen at first, for at one time or another I had seen a deal of trouble coming through gambling. But I thought a little fling wouldn't do me any harm, so I thanked her and asked her to go ahead. If she won, why shouldn't I?"

"Why indeed? And she did arrange it?"

"Yes. I didn't see her for three or four days, then I met her in the train. She said she had fixed up the thing for me and if I would come in early next morning she would introduce me to the man who took the stakes. Our jobs started about one o'clock, you will understand, Mr French, so we had plenty of time earlier."

"Of course. I suppose you both worked on till the places closed in the evening."

"That's right. We were done about eleven or a little later. Well, next morning I met her at eleven and we saw the bookmaker, Mr Westinghouse. Gwen had told me that his office was rather far away and that he would meet us in the Embankment Gardens at Charing Cross. And so he did."

"Now before you go on you might describe Mr Westinghouse."

"I can tell you just what he was like," the girl returned. "You know those big American businessmen that you see on the films? Clean shaven and square chins and very determined and all that? Well, he was like that."

"I know exactly. Right, Miss Darke. You met Mr Westinghouse?"

"Yes. Gwen introduced me and he asked me my name and a lot of questions about myself and he wrote down the answers in a notebook. Then he said he would agree to act for me, but that I was to promise not to mention the affair, as they wanted to keep it in the hands of a few. I promised and he took my stake. It was only five shillings, but he took as much trouble over it as if it had been pounds. He wanted to know if I would like to choose my number, but I said I would leave it to the man on the ground."

"And what was the result?"

"Mr Westinghouse said that he couldn't undertake to let me know before the end of a week, on account of the time it took to write out and back again, and also because the man did not always play, but only when he felt he was going to win. He had a sort of sense for it, Mr Westinghouse said. So I met him a week later. He said I had done well enough for a start. I had won three times my stake. He gave me nineteen shillings, the fifteen shillings win and my five shillings back, less five per cent. I was delighted and I put ten shillings on and kept the nine. That time I doubled my ten and got another nineteen shillings. The next time I lost, but the next I had a real bit of luck."

"Yes?" French queried with as great a show of interest as he could simulate. The tale was going according to plan. He could almost' have told it to Miss Darke.

"That fourth time," the girl went on, "Mr Westinghouse seemed much excited. He said I had done something out of the common and that it was only the second case which had occurred since they started. I had won maximum, that meant thirty-five times my bet. I had put on ten shillings and he handed me sixteen pounds twelve and sixpence!"

"A lot of money," said French gravely.

"Wasn't it? Well, you may imagine, Mr French, that after that I went ahead with the thing. But I never had

15

another bit of luck like that, though on the whole I did fairly well, at least until lately."

That, of course, was the next step. She had still to tell of her loss and the penalty. But that, French felt sure, was coming.

"About a month ago," the girl went on, "Gwen told me she was leaving town. She had got a better job in the Waldorf Theatre in Birmingham. But I carried on the gambling all the same. But somehow after she left my luck seemed to desert me. I began to lose until at last I had lost everything I had won and all my small savings as well."

"And what did Mr Westinghouse say to that?"

"I told him what had happened and that I couldn't go on betting. He seemed cut up about it and said that if he had foreseen that result he wouldn't have taken me on. Then he said it was a real pity I couldn't go on a little longer. The luck at the tables came in cycles and they had been passing through a specially bad cycle. Several other people had lost as well as me. He said the luck was due to turn and that if I could hold on I would be sure to win back all that I had lost and more. I said I couldn't as I hadn't the money and that was all there was to it. He said to let things stand for a week and then to come back to him and he would see what could be done."

"And you did?"

"Yes. Mr Westinghouse told me he was glad to see me as the luck had turned. If I could manage a really good bet he was certain that I should win handsomely. I said I hadn't the money. Then he hummed and hawed and at last said that he couldn't see me stuck; that he felt responsible for me and that he would help me out. If I would undertake to let him have half the profits, he would lend me enough to clear a good round haul. He took two notes out of his pocket and said here was ten pounds. I could put it on in one bet if I liked, but he advised me to put on four bets of two-pound-ten each instead. Someone or two were sure to get home.

"I didn't like the idea, but I was sure he wouldn't have offered such a thing unless there really was a good chance. So after some time I thanked him and agreed. I know I shouldn't have done it, but there it is. I'm telling you just what happened."

French smiled.

"If we were all as wise as we should be, Miss Darke, there would be no stories to tell. Never mind. Just go on with yours."

"Well, you can guess what happened. I lost every single one of my bets! There was I without a penny left and owing Mr Westinghouse ten pounds."

Miss Darke evidently had something of the dramatic sense. She paused unconsciously to give point to her climax, then went on:

"He was very nice about it at first, but soon I saw a different side to his character. He began to press for the money and the more I told him I couldn't pay and asked for time, the more persistent he got. At last, about ten days ago, he said he would give me a fortnight more and that if I had not paid by then he would go to my employers and ruin me. When I said it was his own fault for tempting me to borrow he got furious and said I'd see whose fault it was and for me to look out for myself.

"I was in a terrible state of mind, Mr French. I didn't know what would happen to me or who to turn to. And then the night before last who should I meet going home in the tube but Gwen Lestrange."

Again Miss Darke paused at her climax and French, who had been listening carefully though without a great deal of interest to the commonplace little story, offered a sympathetic comment. How many times had just such a little drama been enacted, and how many times it would again! Probably since before the dawn of history gambling had been used to get fools of the human race into the power of the knaves. There was only one point in the episode still unrevealed — the source of wealth to which this silly girl had access and from which Westinghouse expected to be paid. That, however, would no doubt soon be revealed. For French could not bring himself to believe that it was anything so crude as robbing the till in the cinema, the only thing which appeared to follow from the story.

"Gwen seemed pleased to see me. She said her mother had been ill and she had got a couple of days' leave from Birmingham. She asked me to have coffee with her next morning at Lyons' Corner House, so that we could have a chat.

"I think I told you I started work about one o'clock, and shortly before twelve next day I joined her at Lyons". She exclaimed at once about my looks. 'Why, what on earth's wrong with you,' she cried. 'You're in trouble of some kind.'

"I didn't want to talk about myself, but she insisted on hearing, and when she learned what had happened she was very angry. 'That old scoundrel!' she cried, 'and I used to think he was straight!' She got quite excited about it. She advised me to tell Westinghouse to go to hell and dare him to do his worst. He couldn't do me any harm, she said. I had only to deny the story and say he had been persecuting me and he could produce no proof. But I knew that was no good and that the mere raising of the question with the cinema manager would lose me my job. And it would have, Mr French."

"I daresay it would," French admitted.

"Well, I wasn't on for it anyway, and when she saw I wasn't she let that drop. Then she said that she felt sort of responsible for me, seeing that it was through her I got into the thing, and that she would therefore try and help me out. There was a cousin of hers, a really good sort, who might be able to help me. He had helped her at one time when she was in the same trouble herself. She would stake her reputation that he at all events was straight, and if I wished she would introduce me to him.

"Well, I needn't take up your time by telling you all our conversation. It ended in my agreeing to go to Mr Style, as the cousin was called. Gwen fixed up a meeting. I was to be at St Pancras when his train came in from Luton, where he lived, and he would talk to me on the platform. I went there and he found me at once."

"You might describe Mr Style also."

The girl shivered as if at an unpleasant memory.

"I can easily do that," she said, and her expression became almost that of horror. "As long as I live I'll remember his appearance. He was thin and tall and sallow, with a small, fair moustache. But his eyes were what struck you. He had such queer, staring eyes that would look at you as if they could see right into your mind. They made me feel quite queer. Sort of uncanny, if you understand what I mean."

French nodded and she went on:

"He said that his cousin, Miss Lestrange, had told him of me and the fix I was in, and he thought he could do something to help me. He said he had a job which he thought I could do and which would pay me well. It was easy as far as actual work was concerned, but it required a young lady of good appearance and manner and some shrewdness to carry it through. Also it was highly confidential and the young lady must be above suspicion as to character and discretion. Those were his words as far as I remember."

Again French nodded.

"I said I already had a job which I didn't want to give up, but he said I could do his job at the same time as they didn't clash. It was perfectly easy and perfectly safe, but old-fashioned people mightn't altogether approve of it and that he was glad to know that I had no prejudices in that respect.

"As you may imagine, Mr French, I wasn't very pleased at this, and I asked him rather sharply what he meant. And then he said something which upset me horribly and made me wish I had never seen him. I scarcely like to repeat it."

"I'm afraid you must."

"He asked what I thought of a young lady who betted on borrowed money which she couldn't repay if she lost. Then, always with his horrible smile, he went on to say that a potential thief could scarcely be tied down by out-of-date ideas of morality."

"Plain speaking."

The girl made a hopeless little gesture.

"You may say I should have got up and walked away," she continued, "but I just couldn't. Somehow I felt as if I had no strength left to do anything. But I was terribly upset. I had not realised that I had done anything so serious and I grew sort of cold when I thought of it. He watched me for a moment, then he laughed and said not to be a fool, that I had done what anyone would have done in my place, and that he only mentioned the matter so that I might not imagine that I was above the little weaknesses of ordinary people. I said I never imagined anything of the sort, and he answered that that being so we might get to business."

Though Miss Darke was now telling her story as clearly and collectedly as French could have wished, it was evident that the personality of Style had profoundly impressed her. The more she spoke of him, the more nervous and excited she grew. But French's sympathetic bearing seemed to steady her, and after a short pause she continued.

"He said then that he would make me a confidential offer. He would take over all my liabilities and make me an immediate advance to get me out of my present difficulties. He would also guarantee me a substantial increase to my income, without in anyway prejudicing my present job, if I would do as he asked. He assured me that what he would ask was absolutely safe if I was careful, and that though it might not exactly accord with certain straightlaced ideas, it would not injure anyone or cause any suffering. He also declared on his honour it was nothing immoral or connected with sex. But he said he had no wish to coerce me. I could think the offer over and I was perfectly free to take it or leave it as I thought best."

"A plausible ruffian."

"I asked him then what the job actually was. But he said there was time enough for that, and he began to ask me about the cash at the Milan and how it was checked, and if I was overlooked in the box office and how often the manager came round, and so on. I can tell you I didn't like it, Mr French, and I began to feel I just couldn't have anything to say to his job."

"Yes!" French queried as the girl stopped. "And then?"

"And then," repeated Miss Darke excitedly and with an unconscious dramatic effort, "then he raised his arm and I saw his wrist. Mr French, it had a purple scar like a sickle on the inside!"

CHAPTER
TWO

French Makes an Assignation

If Thurza Darke had surprised French by her dramatic declaration, he surprised her even more by his reply.

"Miss Darke," he said gravely, though the irresponsible twinkle showed in his eye, "you're a born story-teller!"

The girl started and flushed angrily, but he held up his hand.

"No," he said with a smile, "I don't mean it that way. I believe everything that you have said. But I really must compliment you on the way you're telling your story. You did that climax uncommonly well. And I'm not laughing at you either," he went on as her expression changed once more. "I can assure you I consider your statement very important and am following it closely. Go on now and tell me what happened after that. By the way, do you smoke?" He took a box of cigarettes from a drawer of his desk and held it out.

His little ruse succeeded. Miss Darke had become very much excited, and though he liked artistic narrative, he felt it would be too dearly purchased at the price of accuracy. His intervention brought her back to earth. She lit a cigarette and went on more soberly.

"I just sat and stared at the mark while I thought what poor Eileen Tucker had said. This must be the man she had described. I thought of what had happened to her and I shivered with fear. It was clear what her trouble had been."

"Well now, it's not so clear to me. Just say what did you think it was?"

The girl looked at him in surprise.

"I supposed that Style had made her rob the till of the Hammersmith Cinema, and I supposed he would try and make me rob the Milan."

"Not so easy as it sounds," French declared. "But perhaps you are right. Yes?"

"Mr Style evidently saw me looking at the mark, for he seemed annoyed and he covered it up with his sleeve. I felt I had been rude and I looked away. But his manner was not so pleasant afterwards."

"Do you think he had any idea you had known Eileen Tucker?"

"He asked me the question. That was afterwards, after we had talked for some time. Just as I was going away he said: 'By the way, about a year ago I met a young lady in your line of business — a Miss Eileen Tucker. A very nice girl she was too. I suppose you never came across her?'"

"And what did you say?"

"At first I was going to say Yes, then something came over me and I thought it might be safer if I said nothing about it. So I said No, that the name was strange to me."

24

"H'm. Do you think he believed you? Did you hesitate before you answered him?"

"I don't think I hesitated, or not very much at all events. He seemed to believe me all right."

Ugly, thought French. If this somewhat rambling statement were true, it looked distinctly ugly. Indeed Thurza Darke's fears as to her personal safety might not be so misplaced after all. If this Style had murdered Eileen Tucker, Thurza's obvious recognition of the scar would give him a nasty jar. He would realise that she must have heard of it from Eileen herself, and the very fact that she had denied acquaintanceship with the deceased girl would tell him that she suspected him. For the first time French began to think the matter might be serious.

"Before Style asked you if you knew Miss Tucker you say you talked for some time," he went on. "Tell me what you said."

"Not very much, Mr French. I didn't like his questions about the cash arrangements at the Milan, and he saw I didn't. He said he would like an answer from me, as if I didn't want the job he could find plenty of others glad of it. I mightn't like the feeling it was something I couldn't tell my friends about, but that was what the pay was for. The actual work was nothing."

"He made no secret that it was criminal?"

Miss Darke seemed shocked.

"Such a thing never entered my mind," she declared. "The worst I thought was that it mightn't be quite straight."

"Well, what did you say?"

"I said I didn't like it, and he replied that was perfectly all right and that he respected people who said what they meant. Then he got up and said goodbye and began to walk off."

"But you didn't let him go?"

"I didn't," Miss Darke admitted. "While I had been talking to him I had almost forgotten about my debt to Mr Westinghouse. But when I saw him going the remembrance of it seemed to come down over me like a great cloud. I said to myself: 'If I do what Mr Style wants I may be ruined, but if I don't I shall be ruined without doubt.' It seemed the lesser evil and I called him back intending to agree."

"And did you not agree?"

"No. When it came to the point I just couldn't, and I begged for a day or two to think it over. He said certainly, and for me to meet him at twelve o'clock on Friday — that's tomorrow — in the small room to the left of the Turner Room in the National Gallery. I could give him my answer then."

"Well," said French, "there's one thing certain and that is that you've done a wise thing by coming here and telling your story. And you've told it exceedingly well, if I may say so again. Go on, please."

"That's about all there is. I was in absolute misery all that day. In the evening my friend at the boarding house, Jennie Cox, noticed that there was something wrong with me and pestered me so much about it that at last I told her everything. She said I should ask Mr Arrowsmith's advice, but I said I would do nothing of the kind. That was all last night.

26

"This morning about half past ten she came back to the boarding house and said that in spite of my objection she had told Mr Arrowsmith the whole story. At first I was real mad with her, then I saw that Mr Arrowsmith might help me out. So I went to his office with Jennie and told him everything, just as I have to you."

French nodded. For a moment he remained silent, then leaning forward, he spoke with decision.

"Now, Miss Darke, I may tell you at once that you're not to be alarmed about yourself. We'll see you through. But you must do exactly what I tell you."

"You may trust me, Mr French," the girl said earnestly.

"Very well. Tomorrow you must go to the National Gallery, as Style asked you. You will tell him that you have thought over what he said and that you have decided to do as he asked, provided he will give you an undertaking to pay you the money he promised. Don't show any hesitation so far as the moral side of the matter is concerned, but be stiff about the payment. You understand what I'm after? I want him to think he has got you. Finally agree to his terms and say you are willing to start at once."

Miss Darke looked rather scared as she promised.

"Please remember that you have nothing to fear. As a matter of fact you will be watched at the National Gallery by one of our men and you will be perfectly safe. But don't go away anywhere with Style or Westinghouse or Miss Lestrange. Just do as I've said and I'll look after the rest. Now I'll say good day, and again I congratulate you on your wisdom in coming to tell me your story."

That he really was on to something serious, French was now inclined to believe. It was worth looking into at all events, and he determined he would not only follow up Miss Darke's adventures, but also investigate the death of Eileen Tucker.

His first inquiry could be made immediately. Picking up his telephone, he put through a call.

"That the Bijou Theatre in Coventry Street? Scotland Yard speaking. I am trying to trace the movements of a young lady called Gwen Lestrange. She states she was barmaid with you up till about a month ago. Can you give any information about her?"

"Must be some mistake," came the reply. "There never was anyone of the name here."

"She might have been with you under another name," French went on. "She was tall and well built and fair with blue eyes and a heavy chin. Always well dressed — a fur coat and so on."

"No, we had no one answering to that description. Besides, no barmaid left here about a month ago."

French next repeated his inquiry to the Waldorf Theatre in Birmingham. But no one of the name was known there either, nor had a new barmaid been employed within the last four months.

It was what he had expected to hear. Methodically he turned to the next obvious inquiry. Sending the descriptions of the three suspects to the Record Department, he asked if anything was known of them.

28

But here again he drew blank. The gang was not known to the police nor was any of the three an habitual criminal.

So far as he could see nothing more could be done till the next day. He therefore put the affair out of his mind and took up the routine matters with which he had been engaged before Thurza Darke's call.

About 11.30 next morning French, after an interview with his immediate superior, Chief Inspector Mitchell, left the Yard and turned his steps in the direction of Trafalgar Square. As he walked his thoughts were occupied with a revolting and mysterious murder which had taken place the previous evening near Skipton. He thought it not unlikely that the help of the Yard would be requisitioned, and he wondered, if so, whether the case would fall to him. None of the other men, so far as he knew, were disengaged, while he, except for this trifling business he was now concerned with, was at a loose end. He hoped he would get it. He liked the country, especially in summer, and he was getting accustomed to working away from his base. His two last big cases, at Starvel in Yorkshire and down in Devonshire at that Dartmoor affair, had been completed without the help of his staff at headquarters, and he had found little difficulty in working alone.

He reached the National Gallery, and going into the Turner Room, became engrossed in the splendid exhibits hung therein. Though technically ignorant of art, he liked pictures, and of all the pictures he had ever seen, Turner's gave him the most pleasure. The fact that Miss Darke's interview was to take place in the adjoining room did not prevent his making the most of his opportunities before she and her dubious acquaintance arrived.

He moved round, looking at canvas after canvas, and returning again and again to the Fighting Temeraire, which was to him a source of never-ending delight. But all the time he kept half an eye on the door, resolved that when once Mr Style should appear, he should be kept in sight until he reached his office or his dwelling or some place from which he could be picked up again when and if he was required.

Time passed quickly under such pleasant conditions and soon twelve o'clock, the hour of the interview, arrived. But there was no sign of either of the principals. As the minutes slipped away French suddenly grew anxious. Had he bungled the affair already?

He had chosen the room beyond that of the interview in the hope that Style would not see him, so that he could trail him with more ease and security. Now he began to wonder if Style had met the girl at the door and altered the venue to some other room. If so, he might pick them up as they were leaving the building. He therefore strolled to the entrance, and there taking up an inconspicuous position, watched those departing.

For over half an hour he waited, then remembering that Miss Darke began work at the Milan at one o'clock, he concluded his luck was out and went along to the cinema.

It was a fine new building in Oxford Street, not more than a hundred yards west of the Circus. Palatial was scarcely the word with which to describe it, as it was built in a vastly more lavish and ornate manner than ninety per cent of the palaces of the world. French entered a huge hall of marble and gold in which were a row of box offices and from which massive bronze doors led to the auditorium. Only two of the six box offices were open. French glanced into each, but in neither was his friend.

Having learnt from an attendant that though the girl was due for duty, she had not yet arrived, he sat down to wait. Time crawled slowly on. One-thirty came, then one-forty-five, then two, and still she did not appear.

At two o'clock French could stand it no longer. He saw the manager. But from him he learnt nothing. Miss Darke had no leave of absence nor had she sent any apology. She was a reliable girl and had never before missed an attendance. The manager had no explanation to offer.

"I should be obliged if you would let me know at the Yard if she turns up," said French as he took his leave.

He was now acutely anxious. Fears of the worst filled his mind as he drove rapidly to the boarding house in Orlando Street, Clapham.

In a few minutes he was sitting with Mrs Peters, the landlady. At once he obtained news. On the previous evening about half past eleven an attendant had rung up from the Milan. He had explained that Miss Darke had asked him to say that her sister had unexpectedly

31

turned up from Manchester and that she was going to spend the night with her at her hotel.

As a matter of form French rang up the Milan. But the reply was only what he expected. Miss Darke had left at her usual time without giving any message to anyone. Sadly French found himself forced to the conclusion that there could no longer be any doubt that the gang had got her.

The thought of her disappearance profoundly upset him. It hurt like a personal affront. An appeal had been made to him for help. He had promised help. And he had not given it . . .

"They've been too much for her," he thought. "That ruffian Style saw that she suspected him of Eileen Tucker's murder and no doubt he shadowed her to the Yard. He's told his friends that she'll blow the gaff and they've done her in, or I'm a Dutchman."

In accordance with his usual custom he had added a description of his caller to the papers which already formed the beginning of the dossier of the case. It was the work of a few seconds to call up the Yard and direct that an urgent call for four wanted persons should be circulated — those described under the names of Thurza Darke, Gwen Lestrange, Westinghouse and Style in the file in the top left-hand drawer in his desk. Then he turned back and with the landlady's permission made a detailed search of the missing girl's bedroom. But with the exception of a photograph of the girl herself, he found nothing useful.

On his way back to the Yard he called at Mr Arrowsmith's and interrogated Miss Cox, Miss Darke's

32

boarding house friend, once again without result. Nor did a visit to telephone headquarters in the hope of tracing the mysterious call lead to anything.

By the time he had completed these inquiries it was getting on towards eight o'clock. As the hours passed he had been growing more and more despondent. But there was nothing more that he could do that night. By now the description would be in the hands of the police within at least fifty miles of London, and that he had not heard from any of them seemed to confirm his worst fears.

He was just about to leave the Yard when the telephone in his room rang.

"Call through from Portsmouth about that Thurza Darke case," said the officer in the Yard private exchange. "Will you take it, Mr French?"

"Right," said French, an eager thrill passing through him. "Scotland Yard. Inspector French speaking."

"Portsmouth Police Station. Sergeant Golightly speaking. Relative to the inquiry as to the whereabouts of a young lady named Thurza Darke received this morning, I think we have some information."

"Right, Sergeant. Go ahead."

"At about nine-thirty a.m. today a report was received here that the body of a girl had been found in the sea at Stokes Bay, some three miles east of Portsmouth. A party of yachtsmen leaving for a day's sail had seen it floating about a mile from the shore. They brought it in and we had it medically examined. The cause of death was drowning. So far we have been unable to identify the remains or to find out how the girl got into the sea. It looks like suicide. We had already issued a circular when we saw yours. The remains answer the description you give."

"Girl been in the water long?"

"Six or seven hours, the doctor thought."

"Has the inquest taken place?"

"It's arranged for ten tomorrow morning."

"Right, Sergeant. I'll go down tonight, if possible. Wait a moment till I look up the trains."

"There's an eight and a nine-fifty, sir, from Waterloo."

French glanced at his watch.

"I'll get the eight. Can you meet me?"

"Certainly, sir."

The hands of the station clock were pointing to ten minutes before ten when French, armed with his emergency suitcase, left the train at Portsmouth. A smart looking sergeant of police was waiting on the platform and to him French introduced himself.

"The girl was with me on the previous day Sergeant, so I can identify her myself. Otherwise I should have brought someone who knew her."

"Quite so, sir." The sergeant was deferential. "We believe she was a stranger. At least, we haven't been able to hear of anyone missing from anywhere about this district. And your description just covers her. The body's lying at the station, so you'll know in a few minutes."

"Right, Sergeant. Let's walk if it's not too far. I'm tired sitting in that blessed train."

French chatted pleasantly as they stepped along, true to his traditional policy of trying to make friends and allies of those with whom he came in contact. The sergeant was evidently curious as to what there might be in this girl's death which so keenly interested the great Yard. But French forbore to satisfy his curiosity until he should himself know whether or not he was on a wild goose chase.

The remains lay on a table in a room off the yard of the police station. The moment that French raised the sheet with which the head was covered he recognised the features of the girl he sought. Poor pretty little Thurza lay there still and peaceful, her small peccadillos and troubles, her hopes and her joys, over and done with. As French gazed upon her pathetic features, he grew hot with rage against the people whose selfish interests had led to the snuffing out of this young life. That she had been deliberately murdered there could be little doubt.

"It's the girl right enough," he declared. "Now, Sergeant, as you may have guessed, there is more in this than meets the eye. I have reason to suppose that this is neither accident nor suicide."

"What, sir? You mean murder?"

"I mean murder. As I understand it, this girl was in the power of a gang of sharpers. She got to know more about them than was healthy for her and this is the result. I may be wrong, but I want to be sure before I leave here."

The sergeant looked bewildered.

"There is no sign of violence, as you can see," he suggested hesitatingly. "And the doctor had no suspicion of murder."

"There has been no post-mortem?"

"No, sir. It wasn't considered necessary."

"We'll have one now. Can you get the authority from your people? It should be done at once."

"Of course, sir, if you say so it's all right. There will be no difficulty. But as a matter of form I must ring up the superintendent and get his permission."

"Certainly, Sergeant, I recognise that. Can you do it now? I should like to see the doctor as soon as possible."

While the necessary authorisation was being obtained French examined the body and clothes in detail. But except that a tiny bit of skirt had been torn out, as if it had caught on a splinter or nail, he found nothing to interest him.

A few minutes later he and the sergeant were being shown into the consulting room of Dr Hills, the police surgeon.

The doctor was a short man with a pugnacious manner. To French's suave remarks he interposed replies rather like the bark of a snapping pekinese.

"Murder?" he ejaculated when French had put his views before him. "Rubbish! There were no marks. No physical force. No resistance. Not likely at all."

"What you say, doctor, certainly makes my theory difficult," French admitted smoothly. "But the antecedent circumstances are such that murder is possible, and

I'm sure you will agree that the matter must be put beyond any doubt."

"No doubt now. Made my examination. What you want next?"

"A post-mortem, doctor. Awfully sorry to give you the trouble and all that, but Superintendent Hunt agrees that it is really necessary."

The doctor was full of scorn at the idea. He had made an examination of the remains in his own way and that should be sufficient for any layman.

But it was not sufficient for French. He held to his point and it was arranged that the post-mortem should take place immediately.

"A word in your ear, Dr Hills," French added. "Keep the idea of subtle murder before you. These are clever people, these three whom I suspect, and they'll not have adopted anything very obvious."

"Teach grandmother . . . suck eggs," barked the doctor, but there was a humorous twinkle in his eyes at which French could smile back with a feeling of confidence that the work would be done thoroughly and competently.

"He's always like that," the sergeant volunteered. "He pretends to be annoyed at everything, but he's really one of the best and a dam' good doctor too. He'll make that examination as carefully as the best London specialist and you'll get as good an opinion when he's finished."

If time was a criterion, the job was certainly being well done. French, sitting in the nearest approach to an easy chair that the sergeant's office boasted, had read the evening paper diligently, had smoked three pipes, and finally had indulged in a good many more than forty winks, before Dr Hills returned.

"Kept you up, Inspector?" he remarked, glancing at the clock, whose hands registered half past three. "Ah, well, been worth it. Found something. You'll not guess. No sign of murder. No force applied. No resistance made. Death by drowning only. All as I said. *But —*" He paused in his stream of explosives and waited impressively. "But — water in lungs and stomach — *fresh*, Inspector, *fresh*. What do you make of that?"

French was considerably impressed.

"What do you make of it yourself, doctor?" he asked.

"Drowned in the sea. Fresh water in lungs. Pretty problem. Your funeral." He shrugged his shoulders, gave a quick, friendly smile, barked "Night!" and was gone.

CHAPTER
THREE

The Inquest

The problem with which Dr Hills had presented French was not so difficult as it appeared at first sight. There could indeed be only one solution, but that solution carried with it the proof of what French had up to then only suspected, that Thurza Darke's death was the result of neither accident nor suicide, but definitely of murder.

If the water which the poor girl had swallowed were fresh, it obviously followed that she had been drowned in fresh water, her body having afterwards been put into the sea. Why the three fiends had committed their revolting crime in this way French did not know, but it was clear that the placing of the body in the sea could have been done with but one object — to conceal the fact of murder by creating the appearance of accident. And had it not been for the special knowledge which French possessed, it was more than likely that the trick would have been successful.

A further problem immediately arose, trifling in comparison to that of the girl's death, but still requiring a decision. Should the discovery be mentioned at the inquest?

To allow the conspirators to suppose that their scheme had succeeded would have the obvious advantage of making them less careful. In the course of his career French had many times experienced the value of lulling his adversary to complacency, if not to sleep.

On the other hand it would be difficult to keep the matter quiet. The doctor would certainly refuse to hold back such material evidence. This would involve confiding in the coroner and adjourning the inquiry on some technical ground, as that official would not allow a verdict inconsistant with the facts to be returned. But an adjournment would not have the effect desired by French. Until the case was finally disposed of and a verdict of accidental death returned, the murderers would remain on tenterhooks, alert and careful.

Eventually French came to the conclusion that it would be best to let matters take their own course. At the same time he would try to keep out of the affair, so that Scotland Yard's interest in it might remain a secret.

In this case he would not give evidence of identity. His decision therefore plunged Sergeant Golightly into an orgie of telephoning, in order that the inquest might be postponed until he could secure the attendance of Mrs Peters, the deceased girl's landlady.

The proceedings opened in the early afternoon. French had taken his seat amongst the crowd of loafers and other casuals who invariably attended such gatherings, and held no converse with the police. The room was crowded, the affair having produced a mild sensation.

The first witness was a tall, bronzed man of about thirty, named Austin Munn. He deposed that he lived at Lee-on-the-Solent and was the owner of the schooner yacht *Thisbe*. At about 6.30 on the previous morning he and three yachting friends had started off in the *Thisbe* for a long day's sail. They were going east through Spithead and towards Brighton. When they were passing through Stokes Bay, some three or four miles from Lee, he saw something in the water. He was at the tiller and he altered course to pass it closely. When they came near they saw that it was the body of a young woman. They hove to immediately and brought it aboard. They tried artificial respiration for over an hour, though none of them thought it would be any good. The girl looked as if she had been dead for some hours. The body was that on which the inquest was being held. They turned into Portsmouth and on arrival one of his friends had gone to inform the police. The sergeant had come down at once and arranged for the removal of the remains.

Sergeant Golightly stated that about 8.30 on the previous morning Mr Lewis Pershaw, one of Mr Munn's yachting party, reported that his yacht had picked up the body of a young woman when starting out for a cruise. He, Golightly, had gone down and taken charge of the remains. The deceased was dressed in a light fawn coat and skirt, with white silk blouse, flesh-coloured stockings and black patent shoes. She had no hat. On her left wrist was a watch which had stopped at seven minutes past one. She wore a necklace and earrings of imitation pearls. Her face was calm and peaceful.

As a result of his inquiries he had learnt that the deceased was a Miss Thurza Darke, an employee at the Milan Cinema in Oxford Street, London. She lodged in a boarding house in Clapham and the landlady was present and would give evidence of identity. He had been unable to find out how the body had reached the place in which it had been found.

Mrs Peters was then called. She deposed that the remains were those of her late lodger, Thurza Darke. The girl had lived with her for nearly a year. She was quiet and well-conducted, prompt in payment and popular with the other boarders. She, Mrs Peters, had become quite fond of her and this tragedy had come as a terrible shock.

Further questions elicited the fact that the witness believed that her boarder had recently been in some serious trouble. For the last couple of weeks in particular she had lost a good deal of her brightness and seemed to have some worry on her mind. But she had not said anything on the subject and Mrs Peters had not tried to force her confidence.

The witness then told of the telephone call. Though this had surprised her, never having heard Miss Darke mention any of her relations, she had not doubted its genuineness at the time. It was not till afterwards that she had learnt from the police that Miss Darke had not sent it.

The fat was then in the fire. When Mrs Peters left the box Sergeant Golightly was recalled and asked if he had made inquiries into the authorship of the message. His reply that he had ascertained that it had not been sent by any of the officials at the cinema, was the first hint those present had received that the case might not be quite so straightforward as up to then it had seemed. Interest in the proceedings perceptibly quickened and the spectators leant forward and fixed their eyes more intently on the witness. But except to obtain the statement that Golightly had been unable to trace the call and had no idea who sent it, the coroner had no further questions to ask.

Dr Hills was the next witness. He deposed that he had at first made an external examination of the remains, by means of which he had satisfied himself that the deceased had died from drowning. He gave technical details as to the condition of the body, stating that in his opinion death had taken place some eight hours previous to his inspection. That had been made about ten o'clock and this, if he were correct in his opinion, would place the hour of death somewhere between one and two in the morning.

"That would agree with the time at which the watch stopped," the coroner remarked, turning over his notes. "The hands were pointing to 1.07, Sergeant Golightly has told us. Now, Dr Hills, you said that at first you made an external examination of the remains. What exactly did you mean by 'at first'?"

"Last night late the police came to my house. Said they were not satisfied. Had an idea there might be foul play. Wanted a post-mortem. I made it with Dr Carswell."

"And did you find anything which might be taken to support their idea?" the coroner asked, while the recently aroused interest intensified.

The doctor hesitated.

"Found a peculiar fact," he answered. "Outside my province to draw inferences."

"And the fact?"

"Water in the lungs and stomach was fresh."

This statement produced something in the nature of a sensation. The faces of most of those present assumed an expression of bewilderment, but a few seemed instantly to grasp its significance.

"And what," went on the coroner smoothly, "did this fact convey to you?"

Dr Hills shrugged. "Girl was drowned," he declared, "but not in sea. Couldn't have put herself into sea. Body must have been put in by someone else. Least, strikes me that way."

"Did the remains show any sign of force or compulsion?"

"None."

For a moment the coroner hesitated when he had written down this reply, his forehead wrinkled from thought.

"Now, doctor," he said at last, "you know this country pretty well, I take it?"

"Lived here all my life."

"Is there, so far as you know, any river or fresh water area into which this poor girl could have fallen and from which her body could have been carried to the sea where it was found?"

"Don't know of any."

Again the coroner hesitated.

"It must be evident to you, Dr Hills, that your evidence suggests at least the possibility of foul play. I want to ask you now, not only from a medical point of view, but also from your experience as a man of the world, whether you can suggest any explanation of the facts other than that of the murder of the deceased?"

At the ominous word a little ripple of movement passed over the assembly, followed immediately by a silence as those present settled down to listen even more intently. Dr Hills shrugged again.

"Utmost respect; scarcely my province. Since you ask: private opinion: girl was murdered."

"But there is no definite medical evidence for that view?"

"None. Girl was drowned in fresh water. That is all."

The coroner looked round.

"Would any member of the jury like to ask the witness a question before he stands down?"

A small foxy-faced man like a tradesman or small shopkeeper rose to his feet.

"I would like to ask the doctor just what the police said to him about foul play, and then I would like to ask the sergeant just what made him say it."

"That is an important point and one I have already noted," the coroner replied. "Dr Hills stated," he referred to his notes, "that he was asked to make a post-mortem, as the police had an idea there might be foul play. Have you anything further, Dr Hills, to add to that statement?"

"Nothing. That covers everything."

"The nature of the police suspicion was not revealed?"

"No. Not in detail."

"And was the doctor not curious? Did he not ask?" interjected the foxy-faced juror.

The coroner frowned. "The witness has said the nature of the suspicions was not revealed in detail," he said coldly, glancing at the juror. "Were you told in a general way that murder was feared?"

"In a general way, yes. No details."

"Who spoke to you on the subject?"

This was the question French was dreading. If the matter were pressed there would be nothing for him but for him to give evidence.

The doctor looked as if he was going to hedge, then he seemed to think better of it and answered.

"Sergeant Golightly and a representative, as I understood it, from Scotland Yard."

At this a little ripple of movement swept over the assembly. From the spectators' point of view things were going better and better.

"And it was the Scotland Yard man, I presume, who promulgated the suspicion?"

"That is so."

"You may stand down, doctor, but please don't go away. Recall Sergeant Golightly. You didn't tell us, Sergeant, that you had received a visit from an officer of Scotland Yard?"

"You may rest assured, sir, that all the essential facts would have been put before the court. As you know, sir, it is not customary for the police to state the sources of their information."

"I am not criticising your conduct, Sergeant, nor do I wish to embarass your handling of the case, but if there is further information as to how your suspicions became aroused which you can properly give us, we should be glad to hear it."

The sergeant glanced at French. To the latter it seemed that less harm would now be done if he himself gave evidence than if a mystery were to be made of the affair. He therefore nodded and the sergeant replied:

"There is no mystery in the matter, sir. I can tell you everything that occurred. I admit that no suspicion of foul play was aroused by the finding of the body. It seemed to me a case of either accident or suicide. But that afternoon a call was received from Scotland Yard, a general call, sent, I understand, to all stations. This said that a young lady was missing, giving her description and asking for a lookout to be kept for her. When I read it I thought it probably referred to the deceased. I telephoned so to the Yard and there was a reply that an inspector would come down by the evening train to see if he could identify the remains. Inspector French arrived and did so. He said that the possibility of foul play must not be overlooked and suggested that a post-mortem should be made. With the consent of my superiors the matter was arranged. Inspector French then told me who the deceased was and where I should go to get a witness of identity."

"Has Inspector French returned to London?"
"No, sir. He's here."

"Here now? Good. Then call him."

As French entered the box the little ripple of excitement was repeated. A full-fledged inspector of the famous C.I.D. was an unwonted sight in the local courts and people craned forward to see what manner of man he might be.

In the meantime French had made up his mind as to what he would say. He would of course tell the truth, but perhaps not the whole truth. In such matters his conscience was a trifle elastic. He justified his conduct by considering the admirable end for which his evasions were invariably made.

"Now, Mr French," the coroner went on when he had noted the witness's name and occupation. "Will you please tell us all you properly can of this matter."

"There is not much to tell, sir," French replied in his pleasant but respectful manner. "Some time ago I had occasion to visit the Milan Cinema in Oxford Street and I became acquainted with one of the young ladies in the box office, a Miss Thurza Darke."

French, with an admirable air of candour, made a slight pause as if he had reached the end of a paragraph. Immediately he went on:

"Yesterday I was again at the Milan, and I noticed that Miss Darke's place was empty. I asked about her and what I was told did not seem quite satisfactory. As a result I made some inquiries and learned that Miss Darke had left the Milan at her usual time on the previous evening, quite in her ordinary frame of mind and without making any special remark to anyone there. From Mrs Peters, her landlady, who gave evidence here today, I learnt about the telephone message. The fact that the message was a false one confirmed my suspicion that all might not be well, particularly as no reason could be suggested for the girl's disappearance. Considering all the circumstances, it was judged wise to issue a circular that she was missing. This was done and there was a reply from here, as you have heard. I came down and saw that the deceased was Miss Darke."

"And have you any idea as to how her body got into the sea?"

"None, sir."

"What does the fact that fresh water was found in the deceased's lungs convey to you, Inspector?"

"Just what the doctor has said, sir; that she was drowned in fresh water and that her body was afterwards put into the sea."

"Can you account for that in any way other than that the girl was murdered?"

"That is certainly the most probable explanation, though I think there are others. For instance, the girl might have been drowned accidentally or committed suicide, and her body might have been found by someone who feared that he might be accused of murder and, therefore, in a moment of panic, tried to get rid of it in a way that he hoped would keep him from suspicion."

"That doesn't seem very probable."

"It does not, sir, but one has to consider all possibilities."

The coroner continued asking questions, but without learning anything further of interest. Then he turned to the jury and made a short speech. Having surveyed the evidence he continued:

"The questions which you have now to consider, gentlemen, are three in number. First, you have to find the cause of death, if in your opinion the evidence justifies you in doing so. Now to my mind there can be no doubt of this. Dr Hills has told us definitely that it was drowning. Secondly, you have to decide whether this drowning was caused accidentally or whether it was suicide or whether it was murder. Here the evidence is not so direct. It has been established, however, that the girl was drowned in fresh water and the body afterwards placed in the sea, because apart from Dr Hills's testimony, we all know that there is no river hereabouts into which the deceased could fall and in that space of time be carried by the current to where she was found. It is difficult to see with what object this could have been done save that of hiding a crime. If you think that these views are borne out by the evidence you will return a verdict of wilful murder. If on the other hand you consider some other explanation tenable, such as the ingenious one advanced by Inspector French, you may return that of accidental death. If you consider that the evidence points to suicide, you will find accordingly.

"Your third question follows from the answer you give to the second. If you find that murder has been committed you must state, if you can, the guilty party or parties. As to this it appears to me that no evidence of any kind has been placed before you. But here again you must form your own opinion."

Contrary to French's expectation, the jury elected to retire. For half an hour they considered the matter, then at last brought in the verdict which had seemed to him self-evident — wilful murder by some person or persons unknown.

CHAPTER
FOUR

French Makes a Start

"I should like to introduce you to Major Bentley, our chief constable," said Sergeant Golightly to French as they left the courthouse.

The major was a small dark man with a rather Jewish cast of countenance. French had noticed him come in late to the inquest and had imagined he was a police official.

"I was talking over this affair with the superintendent this morning," the major began. "He's knocked up at present and I went to his house. That's why you haven't met him. In the absence of complete knowledge we rather took the view that the key to the matter lay in London and that Portsmouth came into it only as the result of an accidental selection. I should like to know, Inspector, if that's your view also?"

"As a matter of fact, it is, sir. I have some further information which I didn't think it necessary to lay before the coroner, but which I should be pleased to give to you. It tends in that direction."

The chief constable smiled.

"I rather imagined your evidence was, shall I say, bowdlerised. It occurred to me that you were mighty quick in assuming that the girl had disappeared. All the details strictly accurate?"

"Strictly, sir." French smiled also. "But if a meaning other than that I intended were taken from what I said, that would not be my fault, would it?"

"Of course not. Naturally the energies of the police must be directed towards hoodwinking the courts, eh?"

French laughed outright.

"It has its uses," he admitted, glancing with amusement at the sergeant's scandalised countenance. "But this time I fear our adversaries are too wide awake to be taken in by it."

"That so? Well, come along, will you, to the sergeant's office and let's have our chat."

When they were seated and had lit up three of the chief constable's Egyptian cigarettes, French told in detail about his interview with the dead girl and the inquiries he had already made. Both men listened with keen attention and without interrupting.

"What's it all about, Inspector?" Major Bentley said when he had finished. "Those three ruffians get these girls into their power, or try to. But what for? Have you any theory?"

"I've not," French admitted. "At first it looked like an attempt to rob the tills of the cinemas, but all they'd get from that wouldn't be worth their while. It might, of course, be for immoral purposes, but somehow I don't think so. In any case the motive for the second murder is clear. This Style believed that the girl Darke connected him with the first crime, the murder of Eileen Tucker."

"Possibly they found out that she had gone to the Yard and thought she had given them away?"

"That's my view. Probably they shadowed her. If so, they would see that her ability to identify three of their members would make her so dangerous that their only policy would be to make away with her."

"Quite. That's clear enough. But it doesn't explain the first murder."

"It does not, sir. It looks as if there was some game going on to get the cash out of those cinemas, but how it could be done I can't see."

"Nor I." The chief constable shrugged his shoulders. "Well, that's all very interesting, but the point about which I really wanted to consult you is this: If the key to the matter lies in London, as I think we are agreed that it must, the matter is one for you and not for us."

"The body was found here, sir. It is technically a matter for you."

"I know, but that is a detail which can easily be put right. If we apply for help from the Yard you can sail ahead without delay."

"That's true, sir, or at least the Yard can. I should have to report and wait for orders. But as I'm mixed up with the case already, and as I have no other job on hand, I am sure I should be the man sent. Shall I get on the 'phone to the Yard?"

"I think you should. Tell them we're applying to the Home Office for help from them, and that I've suggested that as you're here, you might carry on."

"Right, sir. I'll do it now."

But when French got through to Chief Inspector Mitchell he was surprised by receiving a recall.

"Come and see me first, French, at all events," said his chief. "We'll fix it up then."

French travelled to Waterloo by the 8.06p.m. from Portsmouth, and early next morning knocked at the Chief Inspector's door.

"'Morning, French," Mitchell greeted him. "I was a good deal interested by the summary of those proceedings down at Portsmouth. I fancy there's more in this thing than we've got down to yet. Just start in and give me details of what took place at the inquest."

French obeyed. Mitchell listened without interrupting and nodded his head when his subordinate had finished.

"I sat here," he said slowly, "last night for a solid hour after I had received your telephone, trying to remember a name. At last I got it. Does Arundel convey anything to you?"

"Arundel?" French repeated. "Near Eastbourne that is, isn't it?"

Mitchell's eyes twinkled.

"Eastbourne your grandmother. It's ten miles east of Chichester and some four miles from the coast. That help you?"

French slowly shook his head. "Afraid not, sir."

"Well, I'll tell you. Past that little town there flows a river, the Arun, and in that river one day last October was found the body of a young woman. The medical evidence was that she had been drowned and as there were no signs of violence or other suspicious circumstances a verdict of accidental death was returned. But, French," Mitchell leaned forward and became very impressive, "she was employed in the box office of a big London cinema!"

French stared.

"Good Lord, sir! Another one?"

"Well, what do you think? And there's more in it than that. This girl, Agatha Frinton, was alone in the world, at least no relatives could be discovered; she was living in a boarding house, and the landlady stated that she had seemed very depressed for some ten days before her death."

French swore rather luridly.

"I agree," said Mitchell, the slight twinkle again showing in his eyes. "It looks to me like the last time your friends wanted a recruit for their little scheme, whatever it is."

"That's what I think. It's going to be a big case, this. The further you go into it, the bigger it grows. That's three girls we believe they've murdered and goodness knows how many more there may be that we haven't got on to yet."

"I have a man on that," Mitchell declared. "He's looking up the files. I told him to go for any cases of the death of girls in box offices of places of amusement, including accidents, suicides and murders. That should cover it?"

"That'll cover it all right. But there's another point, sir. We believe they murdered Thurza Darke because they found out that she had been at the Yard and they

56

suspected she was going to give them away. Had this other girl, this Agatha Frinton, been to the Yard?"

"Quite right, French," Mitchell approved. "I have a man on that too. He's making a list of girls who lodged complaints which might apply. There's this girl, Agatha Frinton, and also that other, Eileen Tucker, to start with. But it doesn't follow that they need have actually called here. A first step might have been what Sherlock Holmes used to call oscillation on the pavement. They might have come and looked at the door and their courage might have failed them at the last minute. But if the gang saw them do that it might be enough."

"It would indicate what was in the girl's mind," French agreed.

"True, O king. Now there is another thing. Can we learn anything from the geography of the affair?"

French looked his question.

"Here we have murders taking place at Caterham, Arundel and Lee-on-the-Solent. As geography doesn't seem to be your long suit, hand over the atlas and let's look them up. See," he went on when the places had been found, "when you add London they make a curve: London, Caterham, Arundel and Lee: something like three, four, five and six on a clock. Anything in that?"

French pondered, then slowly shook his head.

"Well, bear it in mind," Mitchell advised. "Later it may give you a hint as to this precious gang's headquarters."

"Then, sir, I am to take up the case?"

"Certainly. Get right on with it at once."

"Very good, sir. I'll go round to the cinema and Thurza Darke's boarding house again now I'm here, but I fancy my best hopes are at Portsmouth. There's quite a chance that they may have left traces when they were getting the body into the sea."

"Quite. It shouldn't take you long to bring them in. You've plenty to go on. You have the descriptions of at least three of the gang and you have three murders to go into, for I think we may take it this Arundel affair was part of it."

"I'll get at it immediately. I suppose," French hesitated, "you've no idea what they might be up to?"

"I'm afraid not. Some way of robbing the cinemas occurs to one at once, but I don't see how it could be done on a big enough scale to be worthwhile."

"That's what I thought. In fact, I don't see how it could be done at all."

"You'll get an idea before long, I fancy. Well, get ahead, French. If you get tied up at Portsmouth you can try Arundel, and if you make a mess of that you can move on to Caterham. Between them all you should pull off the job."

French lost no time in getting to work. Beginning with the boarding house, he interviewed not only Mrs Peters, but the servants and some of the boarders with whom the deceased girl had been on specially intimate terms. Unfortunately, from them he learnt nothing. Nor did a meticulous search of Miss Darke's belongings give better results. Then he drove to Mr Arrowsmith's office and interrogated the typist, Jennie Cox. From her he obtained a good deal of information as to the dead girl's life, but again none of it threw light on his present problem.

By the time he had finished with Miss Cox, the Milan was open, and after lunch he went there to continue his inquiries. Here, after considerable trouble, he learned one new fact, not indeed an important one, but still something.

An attendant whom he had not seen on his previous visit had been on duty in the entrance hall on the night on which Miss Darke had disappeared. About quarter before eleven a young lady had come in. As the show was nearly over he had wondered what she had wanted and he had watched her particularly. She had gone to Miss Darke's box and a short but animated conversation had taken place between the two ladies. He had overheard the stranger say as she was leaving: "Cheerio, then. I'll wait for you at the corner." She was a tall, good-looking girl, stylishly dressed, with a fur coat, and she seemed eager and excited and as if pleased about something. The attendant had noticed also that Miss Darke had hurried away as soon as she could.

In spite of the man's somewhat meagre description, French had little doubt of her visitor's identity. That she was Gwen Lestrange he would have bet long odds. He immediately set to work on the clue. After examining the remainder of the cinema staff, he arranged for the interrogation of the police who had been on duty in the immediate neighbourhood on the night in question, and circulated an inquiry among the taximen of the district in the hope that the girls might have engaged a vehicle.

The great machine of the C.I.D. having thus been set in motion in London, he returned at eight o'clock to Portsmouth. Smoking a meditative after-dinner pipe in the train, he set himself to take stock of the facts which he had already learnt, and to see if they would yield any deductions which might indicate the way in which he should go.

He saw at once that the inquiry resolved itself into two separate and distinct problems. There was the immediate question of the identity of the trio who had murdered these poor girls. For French believed with his chief that all three crimes were the work of the same *parties*. But behind that there was the further problem of motive. What were these three people doing that should lead them to so terrible an expedient?

It did not require much thought to show French that he must concentrate on the first of these questions. Until the criminals were discovered, the second question could scarcely be approached. Indeed, the establishment of their identity might lead directly to the discovery of their motive.

Of the murder of Thurza Darke, therefore, just what did he know?

She had left the Milan at 11.15p.m. in her usual health and spirits, and her dead body was found in the Solent at about 7.00 the next morning. The evidence of her watch tended to the belief that she was murdered at 1.07 and this was supported by the doctor's statement.

French wondered if he could make a provisional timetable of the happenings on that tragic night. Again and again he had found that nothing had so cleared up his views on a case as the fixing of a duration to each incident. Perhaps in this case also it would bring light.

In the first place he considered the time which he should allow for the actual murder. Even with his case-hardened mind he did not care to dwell on the ghastly details. But he felt sure that it could not have been completed in less than half an hour. When he added the time necessary for the kidnapping, he felt sure a good deal longer would have been required. Assume, however, half an hour. 11.15 to 1.07, less half an hour, was about 80 minutes.

It was evident in the next place that the journey from London must have been made by car. There was no train and the difficulties of using an aeroplane would have been overwhelming. Moreover, the fastest motor launch would have taken too long for a sea passage to have been taken.

He had brought a map and guide book of the district and these gave the distance from London to Lee as something like 78 miles. From the above facts, it followed that the crime could not have been committed at Lee. It must have been done within an 80-minute journey from London.

In 80 minutes French thought it unlikely that more than thirty miles could have been done. With such a freight no driver would have run the risk of being held up by the police for speeding. Thirty miles from London in the general direction of Portsmouth brought him to the district containing Wokingham, Aldershot, Godalming, Horsham, and Ashdown Forest. He thought that a provisional assumption was justified that the murder had been committed either in London or somewhere on the London side of this circle.

Some fifty miles had then to be covered. On these country roads a higher speed might be admitted. Still French did not believe Lee could have been reached before about half past three in the morning.

The remains would then have to be put into the sea, an operation which would also have taken time. Suppose it took half an hour. This would have brought the time to four o'clock. About four it would be beginning to get light, and French was sure the criminals would do their utmost to get away as soon as possible from a place with such dangerous associations.

When the train ran into Portsmouth station, French was smiling contentedly. He was pleased with his progress. From nothing whatever he had evolved the definite conception of a car arriving at a point near Lee at some time between, say, 3.00 a.m. and 5.00 a.m. on the morning of Tuesday, the 19th of June, and of the carrying of the body from this point to the sea. Possibly a study of the shore and currents might enable him to fix that point within short limits. If so, it would be strange indeed if he did not find some further clues. In a hopeful frame of mind he put up at the Splendid at Southsea, his plans for the next day settled.

CHAPTER
FIVE

Lee-on-the-Solent

When French woke next morning he found a brilliant sun pouring in through his window. A good omen, he thought, as he gazed out on a sea just as blue and sparkling as the Mediterranean had looked from the Hotel in Nice at which he had stayed when investigating the wanderings of the Pyke cousins. With luck he would make progress today.

A short journey through Portsmouth and Gosport brought him to Lee-on-the-Solent, a pleasantly situated little town of new houses, stretched out along the shore. Five minutes later he was turning in at the gate of Austin Munn's neat villa.

There the first instalment of his luck materialised. Munn, clad in white yachting flannels, was reading the paper on a rustic seat in the shade of a rose pergola. French went over to him.

"Oh," said Munn, getting up. "You're the inspector, aren't you? Lovely morning. Do you wish to see me?"

"For a few moments, if you please."

"Certainly. Shall we sit here or would you rather go into my study?"

"I can't imagine anything better than this. A delightful place you have here, Mr Munn."

"Not too bad on a fine morning," Munn admitted. "Will you smoke, Inspector?" He held out a gold cigarette case. "Terrible business about that poor girl."

"That, of course, is what I want to see you about," French returned, selecting an opulent-looking Turkish cigarette. "The local police have called in Scotland Yard and I've been put in charge of the case. I want to ask you for some help."

"Only too glad if I can do anything, but I've already told you all I know."

"I'm in hopes that you can help me all the same. First I'd like to fix just where you picked the body up. I have an Ordnance map here and perhaps you could mark the spot."

French unrolled the 6-inch map of the district he had brought from London. Munn bent over it.

"It was about here," he pointed, "to the east of Stokes Bay, almost off Gilkicker Point."

"And how far from the shore?"

"A mile, I should say. Not less, possibly more."

"Here?" French made a cross at the place. "Now, how was the tide running?"

"Flowing, but the current was running out. You see, we have rather peculiar tides here. The run in and out doesn't exactly correspond with the rise and fall."

"I didn't know that ever obtained."

"Oh, yes. It's caused, of course, by the configuration of the coast. It's a bit confusing at first. For about two and a half hours after high water the current continues to run up the estuary, though the actual level is falling. Then for some eight hours it runs out. Now on that Monday night it was high water shortly after one o'clock, summer time. After that the tide level began to fall, but the current was still running up towards Southampton. About three-thirty in the morning the current changed and began to run out towards the sea. Low water was about seven-thirty on Tuesday morning, but the current continued to run out for another four hours. That's roughly what happens, though if you want stricter accuracy you would say 'westerly and easterly,' instead of 'up and down the estuary.'"

"I think I follow you. At what time did you find the body?"

"About seven."

"Then if I have understood you correctly, when the body was found about seven, the tide current was running seawards, and had been since three-thirty?"

"That's right."

"Now, Mr Munn, this is where I want your help. Rightly or wrongly I have formed the opinion that the body was placed in the sea at some time between three and five that morning, most probably about four o'clock. Assuming that is so, where do you think it might have been put in?"

History seemed to French to be repeating itself as he asked the question. It was not long since he had sat on the stones at the end of the pier at Burry Port in South Wales and asked stout Coastguard Tom Manners how the tides ran in the Burry Inlet, and where a crate which had been found off Llanelly might have been dropped into the water. If this went on, he thought, he might set up as a tide specialist. He only hoped that today's inquiries would have as satisfactory results as those on that former occasion.

Like Tom Manners, Munn hesitated over his answer, whistling the while under his breath.

"I should say," he replied at last, "a short way above Lee. Perhaps at Lee, perhaps at Hill Head, probably somewhere between the two. It's not easy to say with any degree of accuracy."

"That's good enough, Mr Munn. You see what I'm after? If I search the coast where you suggest I may find some kind of clue."

Munn shook his head. "I rather question it," he answered slowly.

French's eyes narrowed. "Now just why do you say that?"

"I'll tell you. It hadn't occurred to me before, but your question suggested it. I don't believe the body was put in from the shore at all."

"But —"

"I think it was too far out," Munn went on. "I don't mean that the tide runs exactly parallel to the shore. It doesn't. But an object put in at the shore near Hill Head or Lee would not have got so far out from the land in the distance to Stokes Bay."

French nodded.

"I follow you. You mean that the body must have been thrown in at some considerable distance from the shore?"

"Either that or it must have been thrown in earlier and come down from nearer Southampton."

"It couldn't have been much earlier," French objected. "Remember the poor girl was alive and well in London at eleven-fifteen that night." He paused in his turn, then went on: "Any chance of getting a boat along there?"

Munn gave him a sharp glance.

"On compulsory loan? Yes, I believe that would be possible, Inspector. Several of the residents along the shore have boats which lie out at night in the summer. I should think one could be borrowed. But your criminals couldn't get any oars. They're always taken in when the boats are out of use."

"That may prove an additional clue," French declared. "I'm sure I'm greatly obliged, Mr Munn. Thanks to you, my next move is clear. I shall search this stretch of coast in the hope of finding that a boat and oars were tampered with. If I am lucky enough to find them, it may lead me on to something else."

The day was living up to its early promise as he took leave of Munn and set off on foot along the shore. The prospect was charming. Across the blue, sparkling waters of the Solent lay Cowes, peeping out behind the Osborne Woods, while upstream, on the opposite side of Southampton Water, the long, low coastline rose dark and tree-clad from shore to serrated horizon. The sea was dotted with the white sails of pleasure craft, and close under the Island a great liner moved rapidly up towards Southampton. At intervals along the road were villas, opposite many of which were boats. To "borrow" one of these during the hours of darkness should certainly be easy.

But how was he to find out whether or not it had been done? He could see but one way and that long and tedious. He must make house to house inquiries as to whether, first, any trace had been found of the taking out of a boat, and second, if anyone had been heard or seen on the shore about the time in question.

Soon he found his premonition justified. A longer or more tedious job he had seldom tackled. At house after house he called, waited interminably until some responsible person could see him, talked that person into a sympathetic frame of mind and then put his questions. With one inquisitive and voluble householder after another he searched boats, investigated the hiding places of oars and questioned servants. All to no purpose. Nothing helpful was to be learnt. He carried on while the day wore slowly away, growing more tired and dispirited with each fruitless repetition. At last, only one group of houses was left and he began rather despairingly to wonder what he would do if he did not get news at one of them.

But just as he was losing hope the luck turned. In this case the owner was at home and on learning French's business became interested. He had, he said, been shocked to read of the murder and would be glad to do anything to bring the criminals to justice. He at once called the members of his household that French might put his questions. And when this led to no result, he went down with French to examine his boat.

It was moored off the end of a slip. A short painter was made fast to the bight of an endless rope which passed through pulleys fixed to the end of the slip and to a pole driven into the beach some eighty or a hundred feet farther out to sea. This arrangement enabled the boat to be kept clear of slip and pole, while by pulling on the rope the painter could be drawn to the slip. A cord, lapping the parallel parts of the rope at the pulley, prevented accidental movement.

The moment the owner, Mr Farrar, saw this cord he exclaimed; "Hullo! Someone has been here! I never left that cord like that!"

"No?" French answered, his spirits rising with a bound. "How did you leave it?"

"I don't know if you know anything about knots," Mr Farrar went on. "If you do you will see that this is an ordinary clove hitch such as a skilful landsman might make. Now I always use what is called a ratline lock. It was shown to me by a Norwegian sailor whom I once met."

"Pretty conclusive," French admitted. "How long is it since you had the boat out?"

"Must be over a week," Farrar said. "I have been in town for the last four days and I am sure it was four days before that."

"Very satisfactory. Might we have the boat in? I should like a look at it."

Farrar loosened the cord, and pulling on the rope, drew the boat in to the slip. It was about twelve feet long and strongly built and wide in the beam. A good sea boat, French thought.

He got in and began one of his meticulous examinations. Almost at once his efforts were rewarded.

Caught in a splinter of one of the stern bottom boards was a tiny scrap — little more than a thread — of fawn-coloured material. It was just the shade of Miss Darke's coat and skirt and French had not the slightest doubt that it would match the slight tear he had noticed.

"That fixes the matter, I fancy," he said as he put his find carefully away in an envelope. "Part of the dead girl's skirt. I noticed it had been torn. Now let's see if there's anything else."

Never since it had left the builder's hands, if then, had that boat had such an examination as it got that afternoon. But it contained nothing else which might form a clue, nor could French find any fingerprints.

This matter of the boat seemed to him to supply the answer to a question which had puzzled him from the first. If the criminals' object had been to dispose secretly of the body, why had they chosen a landlocked piece of water like the Solent, particularly one so alive with shipping? The answer was evident: the boat. On no part of the open coast could they find boats so conveniently placed for "borrowing." The ease of getting the boat would clearly outweigh the increased risk that the body might be found.

He rejoined Farrar on the slip.

"That's really excellent," he said with ill-repressed delight. "It shows that I am on the right track."

"But I don't see how finding this will help you. There is nothing here to indicate who used the boat."

French did not feel called on to deliver a dissertation on the science of detection.

"It may be a help. You never can tell," was his summary of the situation. "By the way, what about oars? Where do you keep yours?"

"They couldn't have got the oars. They are never left in the boat. We take them up to the house when we've finished with them. The criminals must have stolen oars elsewhere or brought their own."

"One other question. You've told me you didn't see anyone about on that Monday night or hear a car. Now can you suggest anyone who might possibly have been out?"

Farrar shrugged.

"How could I?"

"Well, who are the doctors in this part of the world? Was there a dance in the neighbourhood? You see what I mean?"

Farrar saw, but couldn't help. He gave the names of four medical men, anyone of whom might have been called in by residents in the district. But he didn't know if anyone had been. And then suddenly he slapped his thigh.

"But I do though, after all," he exclaimed. "Findlay's wife had a son that morning! You bet Findlay was out for the doctor. You should go and see him; he's an architect in Portsmouth. Or if you like you can come back to the house and ring him up. I'll introduce you."

French accepted gratefully and in a few minutes the call was put through. Findlay was equally ready to help. Yes, his wife had been confined on the night in question and he had gone for the doctor shortly before four — Dr Lappin, of Lee. But he had met no one on the road nor had he seen a car.

"A call on Dr Lappin seems to be indicated," French declared as he once again thanked Farrar for his help.

"Well," said the latter with a sidelong look, "since you mention it, do you know why I told you about Findlay?"

"Why?"

"For this reason. I know something about the police and I may tell you that you're the first officer who has ever come to ask me a question in what I may call a really civil way. It is generally: 'Tell me or it'll be the worse for you.' But when you treated me as a friend who might be able to help you, why, I thought I'd do it."

"I don't think our people are as bad as you make out, Mr Farrar. But I'm much obliged to you all the same."

After a hurriedly snatched cup of tea, French presented himself at Dr Lappin's door. The doctor was just going out, but he turned back with his visitor.

"Yes," he agreed, "I left here shortly after four. It is about five minutes' run to Mr Findlay's and I should say that I got there about four-fifteen."

"And did you notice a car?"

"As a matter of fact I did. Now, let me see where it was. Yes, I remember it distinctly. It was about half a mile on the Hill Head side of the wireless station, where the road turns inland. I can show you the very place if you wish me to."

"It passed you there?"

"I passed it. It was standing at the side of the road and the driver was working at the engine. He had the lid of the bonnet raised and was bending over it. I slowed up and called out to know if there was anything wrong, but he replied only a dirty plug and that he had got it right."

This was good news. French felt that he was on the trail once more. With his interest aroused to the keenest pitch he went on with his questions.

"There was only one man there?"

"I saw only one. The car was a fairly large one, a saloon. It was not lighted up and there might have been others inside, but I didn't see anyone."

"Was there a moon?"

"No, but dawn was breaking. I could see objects fairly clearly, but no more."

"Now, what about the man outside? Could you describe him?"

"Not well. He was muffled up in a coat and had a soft hat pulled down over his eyes. As far as I could see he was a tallish, thin man with a pale face and a small moustache. But I couldn't be sure of that."

"Anything peculiar about his accent?"

"It occurred to me that he had a sort of inflection in his voice such as you hear in Ireland or South Wales. I don't know about North Wales, as I've never been there."

"High pitched or low?"

"Rather high of the two."

Better and better! If this was not Style, French would, so he said to himself, eat his hat.

"I see. Now, doctor, can you describe the car more fully?"

"I really don't think I can, except that it was a middle-sized, grey saloon. Possibly a Daimler, though really I have no right to give such an opinion. But it seemed rather that shape. Of course, that's the shape of a lot of other makes as well. But I saw the number."

"The number! Why, sir, you did well. What was it?"

The doctor smiled thinly.

"I'm afraid I don't deserve as much credit as you seem to think," he protested. "It happened to be the number of my own car, less one figure. Mine is 7385 and this one was 7395 — one figure different, you see. But whereas my car is registered in Hampshire, this one had a Surrey initial."

"This is valuable information, Dr Lappin," French declared. "Now, before I go, do you think there is anything else that you can tell me? You didn't see anyone on the road, for instance?"

Dr Lappin had not noticed anyone. The facts he had mentioned he was sure of, but he knew no others. When he had returned about seven the car was gone. He promised French to give any evidence that might be required and that in the meantime he would say nothing of what he knew.

On his return to Portsmouth, French drafted a police circular. It was believed that a middle-sized, grey saloon car, possibly a Daimler and possibly registered in Surrey and numbered 7395, had travelled from London to Lee and back during the night of 18th-19th inst. Had anyone seen or heard of such a vehicle? Three persons were believed to have been in the car — here followed descriptions of Westinghouse, Style and Gwen Lestrange. Had these persons been noticed? Had anyone been seen taking out or replacing a boat between Lee and Hill Head during the same night?

From the police station French went to interview the coastguards, but unfortunately without result.

Delighted with the result of his first day's work he went early to bed and slept the sleep of the weary.

CHAPTER
SIX

The Supreme Appeal Court

Though self-congratulation is not precisely the same thing as pride, common experience teaches us that it is usually followed, if not by a fall, at least by a disappointment. French's satisfaction at his rapid progress was no doubt natural, but its sequence proved an illustration of this unhappy principle.

After his first day's achievement there followed a period of stagnation. It was not that he did not show energy and industry. On the contrary, no one could have done more. Rather was it as if the Fates disapproved his frame of mind and withheld the success which his efforts deserved.

And yet the second day began well. On reaching the Portsmouth police station the next morning, news was awaiting him, news moreover which at first sight seemed valuable enough. Shortly before four on the morning of the crime, a motor car resembling in every respect that described in his circular was seen passing through Titchfield in the direction of Lee. It was driving fast, but not fast enough to provoke the interference of the constable who observed it. There being nothing to call the man's special attention to it, he had unfortunately omitted to note its number. But he had noticed on the left running board an object some four or five feet long by six inches in diameter, tied up in canvas and not unlike a bag of large golf clubs.

A second report had come from Fareham. At about five or a little later, a similar car had passed through the town. It had been seen twice, first approaching from the direction of Gosport, and a few minutes later leaving on the road towards Bishop's Waltham. Both the men who had seen it believed that it contained two persons besides the driver, and both had seen the canvas package.

That this car had carried the body of the murdered girl, French had little doubt. It was true that Dr Lappin had not observed the package. But French believed that this was for the excellent reason that when the doctor passed the car it was not there. For he felt sure that he knew what that package contained. In this carefully planned crime, the murderers knew that though they could "borrow" a boat there would be no oars in it. French had little doubt that beneath the canvas cover lay a pair of oars divided into two by some form of socketted joint.

After it had left Fareham, the car seemed to have vanished into thin air. In spite of French's most persistent inquiries, no further trace of it could be found. Nor did a single one of the vast army of men who were on the look-out ever identify anyone as a possible actor in the terrible drama.

The clue of the car number had also petered out, though as French had not expected much from it, he was the less disappointed. Inquiries had shown that that bearing the number seen by Dr Lappin belonged to a well-known Surrey resident of unimpeachable character. There was, moreover, ample proof that the car had been in the owner's garage during the entire night of the crime.

As soon as he was satisfied that every agency which could be directed towards the tracing of the car or the gang was working at highest pressure, French went down to Arundel and made exhaustive inquiries into the tragic death of Agatha Frinton. But though he was untiring in his efforts, he found out nothing more than the local police had already reported.

After a week of fruitless work he transferred his activities to Caterham. Here almost immediately he learned an interesting fact. On the third night before the discovery of the tragedy there had been a dance. The homeward way of one of the guests lay past the quarry hole in which the body of Eileen Tucker had been found. There, at about three in the morning, this man had passed a car standing at the side of the road, the driver bending over his engine. He had stopped and asked if anything was wrong and the man had replied that it was only a dirty plug and that he would have it changed in a few minutes. But though the night was calm he had not heard the car start. Unfortunately, he could not describe the driver, except to say that he was tall and spoke with a rather high-pitched voice.

These facts tended to confirm French's theory that the crime was the work of the same trio as were guilty in the Portsmouth case. But beyond that they helped him not at all. No further trace of the car or its occupants could be found.

Then ensued a period of waiting, heartbreaking to French. In spite of his own efforts and those of his army of helpers no further facts were discovered. No irregularities had taken place in connection with the box office cash at any London cinema. No box office girls had left unexpectedly. Day after day French had to report failure, and each day Chief Inspector Mitchell shook his head and looked grave. "We must get them," the Chief would say. "If we don't, some other poor girl's death may lie on our consciences." To which French could only reply that he knew it, but that everything he could think of was being done.

The strain began to affect his nerves, and it must be admitted that not infrequently "Soapy Joe" was anything but saponacious in manner. Mrs French soon noticed it and it annoyed her.

"What on earth's bitten you, Joe?" she asked one evening when absentmindedness and short answers were all she could extract by a thrilling tale of the delinquencies of the next door neighbour's servant.

"Nothing," said French.

"Nothing," she repeated scornfully. "Don't tell me a pack of lies. You've had something on your mind for the last fortnight. What's the matter?"

"Well," French admitted, "I suppose it's this confounded case. I don't seem to get any forrarder with it. I should have had those three people long before this and I can't get a line on them anywhere."

"I thought it was that. Now, I'll tell you what you'll do. You'll put the thing out of your head and take me to the Palladium. Then when we come home I'll make some tea and you'll tell me the whole story. Telling it like that will perhaps clear it up in your mind and you'll see how to get on."

French did not often bring his business into his home or discuss his cases with his wife. But on certain occasions when he felt utterly up against it he had put his difficulties before her in detail, and it had not seldom happened that she had made some remark or thrown out some suggestion which when followed up had led him to his goal. He remembered particularly one case when she had practically told him the solution of a problem which he himself had been utterly unable to imagine — that worrying conundrum of the identity of the mysterious Mrs X in the Gething murder case of Hatton Garden. Suddenly a wave of hope flowed over him. Perhaps in this case also she would, as he put it, "take a notion."

With a sudden recrudescence of his old energy he jumped to his feet, crossed the room and implanted a whole-hearted and resounding kiss on the good lady's cheek.

"Bless you, Em," he cried. "You're not such a bad old sort. We just will. Come along."

They went along; he, throwing off his depression and in better heart than he had been for many days, enjoying the programme, laughing unaffectedly over the

80

jokes; she, saying little and caring nothing for the show, but full of a tender maternal feeling for this great child in whom all her life was centred.

When they reached home she made the promised tea, but French, with amazing sleight of hand, managed to transform his portion into a glass of whisky and hot water during its passage from the kitchen. He was not a drinker, but occasionally of an evening or if he met a friend he would take what he called "half a peg." This evening somehow seemed to require some such form of celebration.

For, illogical though it might be, he had suddenly become wholly optimistic. Far more than he realised, he was building on the chance of his wife "taking one of her notions."

Presently they began to discuss the affair, she seated and bending over a piece of sewing, he on his feet and moving restlessly about.

"I don't see, Emily, that I can tell you very much more about it," he declared. "I explained it to you before. There have been no fresh developments since then."

"Huh," she returned as she drew back her head and looked critically at her work. "Then tell me again."

Pacing slowly up and down the room, French retold the whole story: the call from Arrowsmith, the interview with Thurza Darke, the checking up of the girl's story, the appointment in the National Gallery which she failed to keep, the search for her and its tragic end at Portsmouth, the crimes at Arundel and

Caterham, and lastly, the means which were still in operation to find the criminals.

To all this she seemed to pay but scant attention, eyes and fingers being concentrated on her work. From her manner, French never could tell whether she was really listening to him or not, though afterwards he usually found she had grasped every detail. When he had finished he waited eagerly for her comment. But she still remained silent, folding and tacking the corners of her work with apparently no thought for anything else in the world. At last, however, she spoke, and as her remark took the form of a question, his hopes bounded up.

"You think those three poor girls were all murdered by the same people?" she said slowly at last.

"Well, don't you?" he answered. "All three were employed —"

"And Mr Mitchell thinks so too?"

"Certainly he does. You see, if —"

"And both you and Mr Mitchell think that they were murdered because they got hold of the secret of this gang?"

"To all intents and purposes, yes. We can't tell whether the girls actually knew the secret, but they knew enough to be dangerous. We think Thurza Darke may have been followed to the Yard."

Mrs French slowly threaded her needle, giving the operation immense thought and care. Then, as if once again able to attend to trifles, she went on:

"If you're right in that, these three are up to something pretty serious. If they would sacrifice three lives to hold their secret it must be either dangerous or valuable?"

"Well, of course, Emily. There can't surely be any doubt of that?"

French was feeling slightly disappointed and a trifle irritated. This was not like his wife. He had hoped for something more illuminating. But he was not prepared for her next question.

"Have they stopped it?" she asked abruptly.

"Eh?" he returned. "Stopped it? Why, that's just it. We have no reason to think so. And that's what's bothering us most of all. If some other poor girl —"

"Because if they haven't stopped it it must still be going on."

"Of course it's going on, or at least we think so," he said impatiently. What did she mean by harping on with these obvious facts? "What's in your mind, Emily? I don't see what you're after."

"Well, if it's going on now, that should give you all you want."

"All I want?" He stared at her with a sudden thrill. Something was going to come out of this after all! "For heaven's sake, Emily, what do you mean?"

But Mrs French was not to be hurried. Deliberately she rearranged her work and started on a new corner.

"Wasn't that Darke girl upset when you saw her?" she went on presently.

"Very much so. She thought she —"

"And she had been upset for some time before you saw her?"

"Yes. She thought those ruffians Westinghouse and Style were —"

"And those other two girls? They were upset too before they disappeared?"

"Yes, I found that both had evidently had something on their minds for a considerable time. The people at their boarding houses and at the cinemas had noticed it. But how does that help? It only means that all three knew they were in a tight place."

"It means far more than that. It gives you all you want so far as I can see."

French swung round in his walk with a gesture of impatience.

"For the love of heaven, Emily, can't you say what's in your mind? How does it give me anything?"

"I've a good mind to let you think for yourself. You're not shining just at present, Joseph French."

He recognised her "way." Though sometimes it exasperated him, he knew that behind it there was only the fondest affection and an intense desire to help. And this time it seemed as if help was really coming. Suddenly thrilled, he answered eagerly: "Don't worry about me, old lady. Get on and let's have the big idea."

"Surely it's simple enough. Cinema box office girls are necessary to this thing. All the girls mixed up in it were upset. It is still going on. Other girls will therefore be mixed up in it. These girls will therefore be upset. Well, find them."

For the second time that evening French strode over to his wife and implanted a hearty kiss on her cheek.

"By Jove, old girl, but you lick creation! It's an idea, that is. Quite an idea." He swung up and down the room, enthusiastic, then hesitated as a wave of misgiving swept over him.

"Well, what is it?"

The phrase about marriage being the domestication of the Recording Angel passed inconsequently through his mind. He hoped his Emily didn't *always* read his thoughts as he answered:

"When those first two girls were put away some crisis in the gang's affairs must surely have arisen. When the business is running normally they may not be upset at all. It may be running normally now."

"Well, if it's running normally there won't be any more murders, which is what you say you want to guard against," she answered dryly. "If murder is threatened, the girls will be upset and that'll give you warning. Don't go out of your way to *make* difficulties."

It was his only chance. As he lay awake that night thinking over the conversation and viewing his wife's suggestion more soberly than in his first flush of delight, he felt that, while unpromising, it offered at least a possibility of progress. At all events he decided that next morning he would begin to work on the idea.

He found his new quest a more difficult job than he had anticipated. There was no use in asking the managers of the various London cinemas whether any of the girls under their charge had lately displayed signs of hidden anxiety. So long as the work was done, the managers would neither know nor care. He must in some way observe the girls themselves.

But this was no more easy. It was out of the question for him to scrape acquaintance with all the cinema box office girls in London. It would take him a year. There must be some quicker way.

At last he decided that inquiries from the door porters was his most promising plan. Accordingly he spent some days going round the cinemas. At each he drew the most likely looking attendant aside and pledged him to secrecy.

"I may tell you," he began confidentially in each case, "that I am a detective from Scotland Yard and that I am looking for a certain girl who has got into the hands of a gang of crooks. You will understand that it is not the girl personally that we're after, but the crooks. Got that?"

The men got it without difficulty.

"We don't know who the girl is, but we know two things about her. First, she is employed in the box office of a London cinema, and second, because of her association with the crooks she will be considerably worried and troubled.

"Now I can't go round all the box office girls in London to see if they are showing signs of mental trouble. And that is where you come in. You know the girls in your box office. I want you to tell me whether any of them have become worried looking lately as if they were in some trouble. That's all."

Upon this the idiosyncrasies of the various men came out. Some were satisfied with the story and immediately gave an intelligent answer. Others required further explanation and much questioning and suggestion before risking an opinion. Still others were suspicious and gave French a lot of trouble before he managed to get their views. Lastly, some were simply stupid. Of these he could make little.

At last after immense labour he obtained the names and addresses of eleven girls, all of whom, according to the porters, seemed to be in trouble of some kind.

His next business was to find out the cause in each case. Here again the problem was horribly difficult. No doubt it could be done by scraping acquaintance with each and in time forcing a confidence. But French had not time for such methods. He had spent long enough on the case as it was and Mitchell was beginning to hint that he would not stand for his remaining on it much longer.

He began by sending a man round the addresses. Five of them were boarding houses. Other things being equal, he believed the gang would select girls from boarding houses. They had done so before and the reason was not far to seek. Girls who were alone in the world were more defenceless and easier prey than those who had a family behind them. Therefore it would be wise to start with these five girls.

Calling at the boarding houses in turn when the girls would be on duty, he asked to see the landladies.

"I'm sorry to trouble you," he began in each case, "but I am making some inquiries about Miss Dash, who, I understand, lives here and is employed in the Asterisk Cinema. I advertised recently for a cashier for my business and she has applied. She seems suitable except for one thing. She gives me the impression of being very depressed and melancholy, as if something was preying on her mind. Now I would not care for a girl of that kind. I called therefore to ask whether you could tell me if her depression is temperamental or whether it is caused by some passing trouble from which she is likely soon to recover."

Like the porters, the landladies reacted differently to this stimulus. One accepted French's statement without hesitation and replied volubly that Miss Dash was the best and brightest of girls, but that owing to the recent death of her young man she was temporarily below her usual form. Another was circumspect, but allowed French to understand that it was believed that the course of true love was not running as smoothly as might be desired. A third was even more discreet, regretting that she was not in the confidence of her young ladies, while the remaining two evidently suspected sinister designs on French's part, and would give away nothing.

He realised that he had not gained much from his visits. Even the first two girls were not out of the running, as, were they in the clutches of the gang, they might easily have invented the stories told by their landladies in order to prevent suspicion attaching to their manner. But this was not likely and French decided that he would first investigate the lives of the other three, those about whose depression their respective landladies would not talk. These were Miss Lilian Burgess of the Cosmopolitan Cinema in the Haymarket, Miss Molly Moran of the Panopticon in

Leicester Square, and Miss Esther Isaacs of the Venetian in the Strand. It wasn't perhaps very likely, but from one of these he *might* learn something.

CHAPTER
SEVEN

Fair Passengers

Once he had decided his course of action, French was not the man to let the grass grow under his feet. On that very same evening on which he had learnt of the existence of the three box office girls, he began his investigation into their lives.

His first move was to warn his helpers, Sergeants Carter and Harvey, for duty at nine o'clock. Promptly at the hour the trio sallied forth from the Yard and turned their steps in the direction of the Haymarket.

"It's in connection with that Portsmouth murder," French explained as they walked. "I want three girls shadowed. We'll do one each. But I want each of you to recognise all three, so we'll go round first and I'll point them out."

The façade of the Cosmopolitan blazed with coruscations of flaming lights as they ascended the marble steps to its doors. Just inside stood French's friend, the porter.

A word from French and he pointed to the pay box over which Miss Lilian Burgess presided.

"Girl in this box is Number One," French whispered, then going to the window he put down a pound.

"Three stalls, please."

The girl dropped out the three metal disc tickets and rapidly laid a ten-shilling note and a shilling on the ledge.

"Could you spare me silver?" French asked her. "I'm short of change."

Without replying, Miss Burgess took back the note and replaced it with a small pile of coins.

The whole transaction was a matter of seconds, yet in the time each member of the trio had carefully observed the young woman and impressed her features on his memory. As they passed into the auditorium and out again into the street via the bar each could have creditably passed an examination as to her face, dress and, to some extent, manners.

"Now for Number Two," said French.

They repeated their proceedings at the gorgeous Panopticon in Leicester Square, where, unknown to the lady herself, they made the acquaintance of Miss Molly Moran. Then they went down to the Strand and similarly "met" Miss Esther Isaacs at the Venetian.

"That's all right until shortly before eleven," French declared. "I want each of these girls followed home. If they meet anyone, get his or her description. I'll do the Cosmopolitan, Carter the Panopticon, and Harvey this place. Here are the girls' addresses. As soon as they get home you may drop it for the night. But I'll want you at eight-thirty in the morning at the Yard. We're carrying on tomorrow."

The three men separated. Harvey suggested that as they were in the cinema they might as well see the programme, and settled down to enjoy himself. Carter was not inclined for pictures and went to look up a friend who lived close by, while French, feeling restless and unsettled, set off for a stroll through the crowded streets.

The air was mild and pleasant as he crossed Trafalgar Square and reached the comparative solitude of the Mall. He sat down on one of the seats to rest after the fatigue of the day, smoking placidly until time, acting through the hands of his watch, called him back once more from refreshment to labour. Then knocking out his pipe he returned to the Haymarket and took up his stand behind one of the great vestibule pillars of the Cosmopolitan. From here he had a good view of the door by which, according to the porter, Miss Lilian Burgess invariably left.

Soon he saw her. She tripped out and ran rapidly down the steps in the direction of Piccadilly Circus. French, hurrying after her, was just in time to see her disappearing into the tube station. He sprinted forward, picking her up among the crowd, and kept behind her as she took a south-bound Bakerloo train. From the next compartment he kept her in view, and when she passed out of the Elephant station he was within twenty feet of her. She led the way down New Kent Road, straight to her address in Theobald Street.

As far as that evening was concerned, therefore, he had drawn blank. He did not think she would reappear that night, so after waiting on chance for a few minutes, he went home.

After interviews with Carter and Harvey next morning, at which he learnt that their experiences had been precisely similar to his own, the shadowing was resumed. As the three girls did not begin work until one o'clock and were kept late at night, it was unlikely that they would be early risers. Nevertheless, French was leaving nothing to chance and before nine he and his lieutenants were at the scenes of their various labours. In French's case there was a rather shabby restaurant across the road from Miss Burgess's boarding house and there, hidden behind the dilapidated window blind, he toyed with breakfast and watched the street. But he had to read the paper very thoroughly and smoke a number of pipes before he saw his quarry. No less than two hours passed before she left the house and walked in a leisurely way down the street. French, in an even more leisurely way, walked after her.

She went straight to Westminster Bridge Road, crossed the river, and passing through into Great George Street, entered St James's Park. At a steady pace she crossed the Mall and the Green Park and reached Hyde Park. There she went up one side of the Serpentine, round the top at Bayswater Road, and down the other side to Hyde Park Corner. French had fallen far behind, but when he saw her start off along Piccadilly, he closed up and kept about twenty feet off. She led him along Piccadilly to the Circus, then turning down the Haymarket, she disappeared into the Cosmopolitan.

In spite of the fact that he had been expecting some such *denouement*, French swore. There was his whole morning gone and nothing to show for it! He had an accurate knowledge of where the young lady had taken her morning exercise, but that was all he had learnt. It looked as if he was on the wrong track and that this girl at least had no connection with the gang.

But such had not been proved. It would require a much longer and more detailed investigation to set the point at rest. Shrugging his shoulders, he went back to the Yard to hear how Carter and Harvey had fared.

He overtook Harvey at the door. Miss Isaacs had spent her morning in a very similar way to Miss Burgess. She had left her boarding house about eleven a.m. and gone for a walk. Harvey had kept her in sight during the whole period and was satisfied that she had not communicated with any other person.

In a few minutes Carter came in. Molly Moran had left her boarding house in Nelson Street, a small street running between High Street and Arlington Road, at 11.30 a.m. She had taken a Hampstead and Highgate train at Mornington Crescent station and had travelled to Charing Cross. On emerging from the station she had strolled slowly about, first under the Southern Railway bridge, and then up and down Craven Street. Carter had had considerable difficulty in keeping her under observation without revealing his objective. But he had imagined that she was waiting for someone and had not let her out of his sight for a moment.

After about ten minutes, a grey saloon car had come quickly down the street, and pulling in to the pavement, had stopped beside Miss Moran. She had immediately jumped in and the car had swung off towards the Strand. Carter had raced for a taxi. By a stroke of luck he had got one without having to go to the rank under the bridge, and when he had reached the Strand the

94

grey car was still in sight, circling Trafalgar Square. But his luck had then given out. In the press of traffic his taxi had been held back, and by the time it had got free the quarry had disappeared up Cockspur Street. After fruitless attempts to find it, Carter had driven to Leicester Square and taken up a position from which he could watch the doors of the Panopticon. In some forty minutes Miss Moran had arrived, walking slowly. As it was then twenty minutes to one, Carter had assumed that she would not again leave the building, and had returned to the Yard.

"What was the number of the car?" French asked.

"MX1382. As far as I could see it answered the description of the one you heard of in Hampshire."

French nodded.

"I was going to ask you that. Did you see anyone in it?"

"Only the driver. I couldn't see him clearly through the glass, but he seemed a big, stout, clean-shaven man. He wore a soft felt hat; looked like grey, but I couldn't be sure of the colour."

"Did the girl get in beside him?"

"No. She didn't seem speak to him, but jumped in behind and he drove off at once. The thing seemed arranged and they hurried through it as quickly as possible."

This hurry seemed significant to French. Moreover the driver was suggestively like Thurza Darke's description of Westinghouse.

"Same thing tonight and tomorrow morning," he said to his satellites, "only that we'll change round. We

95

don't want those girls to spot that they're being shadowed. You, Carter, can take the Isaacs girl and Harvey Miss Burgess and I'll shadow this Molly Moran."

That night the three young women went quickly home as before, and next morning at nine o'clock French found himself trying to kill time unostentatiously in Nelson Street until Miss Moran should take it into her rather pretty head to sally forth on the day's adventures. There was here no convenient restaurant and he found himself hard put to it to keep an eye on the boarding house without attracting the attention of the curious. But French was an expert at his job, and by buying innumerable boxes of matches and cigarettes at the neighbouring tobacconists and making indefatigable inquiries for one, Mrs Entwhistle, a mythical dress-maker whom he had invented for the occasion, he contrived to fill in the time.

At just half past eleven, the same hour as on the previous day, the young lady in question emerged from the boarding house and turned her unhurried steps towards Mornington Crescent tube station. Again she took a south-bound train. French expected that she would alight at Charing Cross as before, but she nearly gave him the slip by jumping out of the train just before it started from the Strand. However, he managed to follow her, and when she reached the courtyard of the main line station he was not more than ten yards behind.

Determining that he should not be left in the lurch like Carter, he engaged a taxi, telling the driver to follow the young lady in blue. The man, allowing himself the suspicion of a wink, started off as if the following of pretty young women was a matter in which he had considerable experience. Whether or not this were so, he performed his task with practised skill, stopping at times to adjust his engine or ask a direction or allow French to buy a paper, so as to keep his speed down to that of his quarry's.

The chase led across the Strand and up Chandos Street, and there at the quiet end next Bedford Street the previous day's performance was repeated. Miss Moran walked slowly up and down until suddenly a grey saloon car appeared, drew in to the footpath beside her, and stopped. It was driven by an elderly, clean-shaven man of the successful American business type. So far as French could see it contained no one else. Miss Moran stepped quickly forward and got into the tonneau and immediately the vehicle slid away.

"Follow the car," French told the driver.

The journey was short. From Chandos Street the grey saloon turned up Bedford Street and into Garrick Street. There it stopped and Miss Moran got out. Immediately it drove quickly away.

"After the car," cried French. "Never mind the girl."

But just as Carter had been held up on the previous day, so now French's luck deserted him. The grey car, passing along Cranbourne Street, just crossed Charing Cross Road when the officer on point duty closed the road and French was held up.

Seeing that to follow the car was out of the question, he was about to shout to his man to try to find the girl again, when glancing through the back window, he saw her approaching. He therefore paid his man off and, when she had passed, slipped out of the taxi and followed her.

But she merely walked on aimlessly through the streets, evidently killing time, until some forty minutes later she reached Leicester Square and turned into the Panopticon.

French walked slowly back to the Yard, pondering over what he had seen. The whole proceeding was certainly very suggestive. He didn't believe there could be any innocent explanation. Something shady, he felt sure, was in progress.

Next morning he had another try. This time he waited at Mornington Crescent and picked up Miss Moran as she was entering the train. He followed her to Charing Cross, where she changed and took an East bound Circle train to the Temple. There she got out, and turning away from the river, began pacing up and down Norfolk Street. French hailed the first taxi he saw, and instructing his man as before, sat back in it to await events.

In about five minutes he saw the proceedings of the previous day repeated. The grey car appeared, driven, as far as he could see, by the same man. It picked Miss Moran up, crossed the Strand, and passed up Aldwych and into Kingsway. Then turning down a street to the left, it ran into Wild Street. There the young lady got out.

French had told his driver what to expect, and as the grey car ran on into Drury Lane, French's vehicle was close behind. Through Broad Street and High Street it passed and then along Oxford Street to North Audley Street, down which it turned. And then in Grosvenor Square the whole thing was repeated.

On the footpath in Grosvenor Square stood a young woman. French could not see much of her, but he noticed that she was well dressed and that her bobbed hair was flaming red. The car stopped, she jumped into the back seat, and once again the car swung on.

More interested than ever, French continued the chase. The grey car passed on down South Audley Street and along South Street into Waverton Street. There it stopped and the girl got out, the car turning on down Charles Street.

For a moment French hesitated as to which of his two quarries he should follow. He would have given a good deal not to have been playing a lone hand at that moment. Rightly or wrongly he decided on the car.

Once again to his amazement a similar scene was enacted. From Charles Street the car ran by Berkeley Street, Piccadilly, Grosvenor Place and Vauxhall Bridge Road to Tachbrook Street. There another girl was waiting who in her turn jumped into the back of the car. She was driven through Bessborough Street to Grosvenor Road, and set down at the end of Page Street.

Still another time French followed the car and still another time the same thing happened. A fourth girl was picked up in Darwin Street, off the Old Kent Road and near Bricklayers' Arms Goods Station. She was taken to Long Lane in Bermondsey and there set down, while the car went on to Newington Causeway.

French began to wonder if the whole day was to be spent in giving rides to girls. It was now nearly one, the hour at which most of the cinemas opened, and if the girls picked up were engaged in cinema box offices there would scarcely be time to deal with any more. With keen interest he settled back in his taxi, anxious to learn the next development.

But this fourth girl, it turned out, was the last. The grey car ran westwards till it reached Waterloo. There it turned to the left into York Road and again to the right into a narrow street labelled Tate's Lane, disappearing finally into a gateway about half-way down the street. French's car ran on past the gateway, and turning into the cross street at the end of Tate's Lane, stopped. Telling his driver to keep him in sight, French walked back to the corner and watched the gateway.

He had noticed as he came past that the latter was surmounted by a signboard bearing the legend "Thos. Cullan, Coachbuilder." A glimpse through the open gate revealed a dilapidated yard in which stood a number of carts and lorries. Evidently Mr Thos. Cullan was not in too successful a way of business. French wondered if the man he had shadowed was Mr Cullan himself. At first he thought not. That untidy, ineffective looking yard did not accord with the forceful, decided, face of the driver of the car. Then he saw that if the business with the girls was the serious factor in the man's life, coach building might be merely a blind to mask his other activities.

For fifteen minutes or more French hung about the corner. Then the man appeared, well dressed and prosperous looking, and set off striding with assured steps down the lane to York Road. He turned to the right into Waterloo Road, and French had to sprint at his highest speed to avoid losing him at the corner. He was just in time to see him disappearing into the station, and with a rapidly increasing sense of satisfaction he followed him to the restaurant.

At opposite ends of the big room French and his quarry lunched, then the chase was once more resumed. This time the trail led down Waterloo Road, past the Old Vic. and into Webber Street, where the man vanished into a doorway.

French hung back until he thought the coast was clear, then lounged forward and entered also. The doorway led into a dilapidated passage with a flight of stairs rising at the end to offices above. On the jambs were the names of the occupants. Seven persons or firms French counted. There were two solicitors, an estate agent, an engineer and architect, a commission agent, a wholesale tea merchant and a firm of electrical suppliers. Having noted the names, French passed back to the street and took up a position from which he could keep the entrance in view.

For an hour he waited, sitting in his taxi for the most part, while the driver busied himself with his engine. Then suddenly the quarry reappeared and strode off in the same forceful and determined way. French shadowed him to Waterloo and down to the Bakerloo tube. Booking to Watford, which he thought should cover any journey that the unknown might make, French followed him to the platform. The man took a north-bound train and French, slipping in his usual way into the next carriage, settled down to await developments.

At Harrow the man got out. French noted that he was evidently a "season" and a man of some standing, for the ticket collector touched his cap respectfully. He turned out of the station on the down side of the line and set off towards the Hill.

"Can you tell me if that is Mr Pointer?" French asked the collector as he gave up his own ticket.

"No, sir. Welland is his name."

Curtice Welland, Commission Agent, was one of the names on the office door in Webber Street. So far, so good.

On these comparatively deserted roads, shadowing was no easy task. French had to drop a long way behind to avoid attracting his quarry's attention. Every time the man turned a corner French was therefore at a disadvantage, and had to run to reach the cross road before the other disappeared from view. This again brought him too close and he had suddenly to loiter until the necessary distance again intervened — a by no means unobtrusive mode of progression.

The last turn led into a recently made road. Its end, in fact, vanished into the fields and fresh earthwork showed that it was in process of being extended. The houses along it were all quite new. Several were unfinished, while a few vacant building lots still remained.

About halfway down on the right were a couple of small semi-detached houses, mere bungalows. Into one of these the man turned, letting himself in with a latchkey.

French was approaching a cross lane, and down this he immediately turned. So far he felt satisfied with his progress. The man, he was sure, had not seen him. Now he must find some cover from which he could keep the house under observation.

Right at the end of the unfinished portion of the road, a couple of hundred yards beyond the house, he had noticed a small clump of low-growing trees. He thought if he could reach this it would suit his purpose.

Passing down the cross lane to the back of the row of houses, he came into open fields. These were separated by thorn hedges, one of which ran parallel to the street. French crept along behind the hedge until he came to the clump. There he found that while himself completely hidden from view, he had an excellent view of the house.

He lay down at his ease on the soft grass, and taking out his pipe, began a leisurely smoke. It was a perfect summer's day, warm and balmy, with a bright sun, a brilliantly blue sky and in the distance a few faint, fairy-like streaks of cirrus cloud. The meadow behind him had recently been cut and the soft breeze bore a delightful scent of fresh hay. The air was quivering with the songs of birds, with as a pedal bass the hum of innumerable insects.

It was all so peaceful and soporific that after a few minutes French deliberately sat up in a somewhat strained position lest he should fall asleep and miss his quarry.

Up to the present he had been too busy to think over what he had seen, but now he began to turn the facts over in his mind. That he was on to some very peculiar happenings there could be no doubt, but as yet there was no evidence to show that these were criminal. Still less was there proof that they were connected with the murders. But he was at least satisfied that the affair was sufficiently suspicious to warrant further investigation.

What, he wondered, could be going on? It looked as if the unknown man had an interview each day with each of these four girls. This, of course, was not proved, as you could not argue to the general from two days' experience. But it seemed likely, and if so, what could be the object of these interviews?

It was improbable, he thought, that the man could be interested in the girls themselves. Rather he imagined that they must represent channels by which something was passed between the man and still other unknowns. Whether that something was material, such as stolen goods or money, or whether information was being conveyed between the members of some organisation and headquarters, he could not imagine. In any case it was desirable that Scotland Yard should know more about it.

It would not be his fault, he resolved grimly, if before long Scotland Yard did not know all there was to be known.

CHAPTER
EIGHT

The Grey Car's Round

The remainder of that day came to French as a sort of anti-climax. He put in a wearisome afternoon's work with, so far as he could see, no result whatever.

After some half-hour in the clump of trees he suddenly saw his man appear at the door of the house, wearing plus fours and with a bag of golf clubs over his shoulder. He turned towards French and when he reached the end of the road, struck off along a footpath across the fields. This brought him near French's retreat, not so near as to risk discovery, but near enough to allow French to fall in behind him with the minimum of trouble.

The chase lasted for nearly a mile, the quarry striding easily along as if he enjoyed the walk. At last they reached the links for which the other had been aiming. Welland disappeared into the club house, emerging a few minutes later with a companion. The two strolled to an adjoining green, teed off, and in a leisurely way followed the balls.

That a round of golf offered a favourable opportunity for the interchange of small objects or of confidences between conspirators, French was well aware. He therefore hesitated as to whether he should try to keep the men in view with the object of seeing whether they acted suspiciously and of learning the identity of the partner. Eventually he decided that the game would probably prove to be a side issue, and that he would be better employed in finding out as much about Welland as he could.

Returning to Harrow, he called at the police station and asked the sergeant for information

"I can't give you much, I'm afraid, sir," the man answered, "but if you can wait a little, I'll make a few inquiries." He called a subordinate. "Here, Colgate, you know that man Curtice Welland, of 39 Acacia Avenue? Isn't his housekeeper a local?"

"Yes, sir. Sister of Jaques, the confectioner."

"I thought so. Then go down to Jaques and pick up anything you can about Welland. Quietly, you understand. Or would you rather go yourself, Mr French?"

"No," said French, "I'm supposed to be shadowing the man himself. I left him on the links and I'll get back there."

"Very good, sir. Nothing wrong, I hope?"

"I don't know yet. He's been acting suspiciously, but it may not amount to anything. Well, Sergeant, I'll call in later on for your man's news."

Arming himself with a packet of raisins and chocolate, French returned to the approach road to the golf links and settled down to wait his man's appearance. It was nearly seven before he saw him and then the earlier proceedings were reversed. French shadowed him back to his house along the path over the fields. Once more French hid in the clump of trees and once more he settled down to watch.

Fortunately, the magnificent day had turned into an equally delightful evening or French's lot would have been less pleasant than it actually proved. Hour passed after hour and Welland made no sign. Hungrily French consumed the last fragments of his raisins and chocolate and slowly smoked pipe after pipe. As it grew dark he left his retreat and drew nearer and nearer the house. But his man remained hidden, and when half past ten arrived he decided that nothing more was to be learned that night and gave up his vigil.

On his way back to town he called at the police station to learn the result of the pumping of Jaques. It had not proved very successful. All that the sergeant had discovered was that Curtice Welland had come to the neighbourhood some twelve months previously, buying the house in which he lived. He was believed to be well-to-do, for though he had some job in town and went in every day, he was able to get home early and to play a lot of golf. Apparently he was unmarried, at least no woman other than his elderly housekeeper had been seen about the place. He lived a retired life, going out but little in the evenings and doing practically no entertaining. He took no part in the public life of the place, but he was understood to be popular among the golfing set and to be generous in the matter of subscriptions to charity. So far as the sergeant knew he was not connected with any church or other local organisation. He went to town daily by the 9.17 a.m. train and usually returned about four p.m.

With this French had to be content. Admittedly it did not back up his suspicion that the man was a criminal. But he reminded himself that if a criminal were wishing to lie low he would comport himself in just such a way.

Next morning French had three helpers, Carter, Harvey and a third man called Pickford. At 9.17 they boarded the Bakerloo train at Harrow, having first seen Mr Curtice Welland seat himself in a first-class carriage. They were close behind him when he left the train at Waterloo and separately followed him to his office in Webber Street. There he disappeared, while the four made themselves as inconspicuous as possible, French engaging a taxi to wait within call.

About eleven their man appeared and strode off in his slightly important, prosperous looking way. He followed the route he had covered on the previous evening until he reached York Road and Tate's Lane. The coachbuilder's yard gate was open and he turned in and was lost to view. French and his helpers thereupon got into their taxi, and making a circuit through the neighbouring street drew up at the far end of Tate's Lane, ready to follow the saloon car should it make its appearance.

For half an hour they waited, which suggested to French that Welland did his own chauffeuring. Then the grey car came slowly out of the yard and turned towards York Street. Immediately the taxi followed. The chase led northwards. Over Waterloo Bridge it passed into the Strand, and turning to the right through King William Street, led into Orange Street. There the proceedings of the previous day were repeated. On the footpath stood Molly Moran. The car drew in opposite her, she stepped into the tonneau and the car drove off. It turned into Whitcomb Street, crossed Coventry Street, and in Wardour Street stopped. Miss Moran got out and it drove on.

French's bewilderment was reflected in the faces of his companions as the taxi followed. This thing, whatever it was, happened day after day and was apparently carried out on a definite system. For four consecutive days Welland had picked this girl up in his car, carried her for a few hundred yards and set her down again. Each day it was in the same part of London, but in a different street. What could the object be?

As on the previous day the car now drove westward. Its second stop had been in Grosvenor Square. This time it stopped in Berkeley Square, five minutes' walk away. There the girl with the red hair was waiting. She jumped in and two minutes later, in Grafton Street, jumped out again, while once more the car drove off.

"Now, Carter, your shot. Follow her," French directed and Carter, slipping out of the taxi, vanished.

The third girl, who had been picked up in Tachbrook Street on the previous day, was waiting in Rochester Row, scarcely five minutes away. She had a three minute run, alighting in Regency Street. As she walked off, Harvey slouched after her. Then the car crossed the river and stopped for the fourth girl in Upper Grange

Road, again close to Bricklayers' Arms station. She and Sergeant Pickford got out five minutes later, while French cautiously trailed the car back to Tate's Lane and Mr Curtice Welland from there to his lunch and then to his office.

Shortly before three Welland reappeared and walked, precisely as on the previous day, to the tube station at Waterloo. After a momentary hesitation French, on seeing him enter the Harrow train, gave up the chase. He thought he could do better elsewhere.

He returned to Webber Street, and mounting the stairs, took quick stock of his surroundings. The house was five stories high and on each upper floor were two sets of tiny offices. "Curtice Welland, Commission Agent," was housed on the third floor, with "Harold Tozer, Engineer and Architect," opposite. The whole place was dirty and dilapidated and suggestive of unprofitable business.

French approached Welland's door and knocked. There was no response. Guardedly he examined the lock. It was old and he thought it might prove amenable to the persuasion of a bent wire. But obviously he could not attempt any burglarious exploits at the moment, even if sounds of movement in the engineer's office had not warned him off.

For a moment he paused, then crossing the landing he knocked at the engineer's door. A lanky young man opened.

"Sorry to trouble you," French apologised, "but I am looking for a Mr Fairchild, an engineer. I'm afraid I've been misdirected. Do you by any chance know him?"

"No," said the young man, "there's no one of that name here. Sorry I can't help you."

French replied conventionally and retreated down stairs. He had obtained the look at the occupant of the engineer's office which he had wanted. Moreover, he had seen enough to convince him that the young man was alone.

Once again he took up his weary vigil in the street below. For nearly an hour he killed time before he saw his new acquaintance leave. Then he quickly re-entered the building and climbed to Welland's office.

With considerable misgiving he had determined to do a dangerous and prohibited thing — to search the premises without a warrant. He felt sure he could do so without discovery. The whole of the floor itself was unoccupied, and the wooden steps of the stairs would give plenty of notice of anyone's approach. Unless some extraordinarily unfortunate accident should bring Welland himself back, he should be quite safe.

As an additional precaution he knocked once more on both Welland's and Tozer's doors. When he had waited a moment he clattered down stairs, then creeping silently up again, he took his bent wire from his pocket and set to work on the lock. In a very few moments it yielded to his treatment, and passing softly through the door, he closed it behind him.

The room was fitted up in the barest way as an office. In the centre stood a roll-top desk with an Austrian bent wood chair behind it. A second chair faced the desk. In one corner was a cupboard of painted deal. And that was all. There was not even a blind on the window, nor a waste paper basket. And the second room was entirely empty.

The doubt of the commission agency business, which all this suggested, was increased by a rapid search of the desk. It contained only some financial newspapers, a notebook with records of stock and share transactions, and a number of novels of the more modern and intellectual type. The cupboard, which was not locked, was empty.

In spite of the speed at which French worked, his search was amazingly thorough. Every leaf in the notebook was turned over and its contents examined, every novel was gone through lest letters or loose sheets might have been left between the pages, the walls and floor were examined for secret hiding-places. In short, when he concluded that there was nothing in the rooms to interest him, it was because he had made absolutely certain of the fact.

Only once had he had a bad moment, when he had heard laboured steps ascending the stairs. Silently he had withdrawn to the inner room, in the hope that even were it Welland, he might still escape discovery. But the steps had passed on to one of the offices above, and again breathing freely, he had resumed his work.

In his withdrawal also he was fortunate. Having looked round to make sure that no signs of his visit remained, he drew the office door silently after him, and gained the street unseen.

It was by this time after six o'clock and French felt that he had done enough for the day. But he went back to the Yard, not only as a matter of routine, but to receive the reports of his three men.

For the first time since he returned from Portsmouth French felt a sudden thrill of delightful excitement as he listened to those reports. It looked as if at long last he really was on the right track. For each of the three girls was employed in a box office!

The red-haired girl, it seemed, worked in the Royal Cinema in Edgware Road and the other two in theatres in Vauxhall Bridge Road and Old Kent Road respectively. Each had walked from the point at which she had been set down to her place of business, directly or by a circuitous route, as was necessary to bring her there at the required time. None of them had held any communication with any other person during the walk. In each case the shadower had found out his quarry's name, but not her address, as all three men were afraid of calling attention to their activities by too persistent questioning.

"Well," said French, "get back again this evening and shadow them home."

Though French himself had been looking forward to a quiet evening in the bosom of his family, his eagerness was now so great that after supper he sallied forth once more to try to push the case a step further. After considerable trouble he succeeded in obtaining interviews with the managers of all four places of amusement — the two cinemas and the two theatres. To each he explained his official position, and having made it clear that nothing was suggested against the girls personally, he put his questions.

But as he had foreseen, the managers were not helpful. None of them had noticed anything abnormal or suspicious in the conduct of the girl in his company's employment, nor had there been any irregularity about her cash.

Next day French carried his routine inquiries a step further. Armed with the addresses which his three assistants had discovered on the previous evening, he interviewed the landladies of the three new girls' boarding houses. In each case he was assured that the girl in question had been in evident trouble during the previous six months. But the landladies did not think it was financial. At least none of the girls had shown a difficulty in meeting her bill.

The result of these inquiries left French more than ever determined to probe the affair to the bottom. But when he came to consider his next step he found it was not so obvious. At last he decided to get hold of the girls one by one, and try to force a confidence. This of course had the serious drawback of being a virtual warning to the gang that the police were on their track, but he could see no other way that held out so promising a result.

CHAPTER
NINE

French Makes a Second Assignation

About ten o'clock next day French knocked at the door of No. 27 Nelson Street, and sending in a card inscribed "Mr Joseph French," asked if he could see Miss Molly Moran.

He sat waiting in the plain, somewhat comfortless sitting-room until after some minutes the girl he had shadowed entered.

"Miss Moran?" he asked with his pleasantest smile. "My business will not take long. Will you sit down, please?"

She was a prettier girl than he had realised. Rather below middle height, she had a graceful figure, with small shapely hands and feet. Her hair and eyes were dark, her nose tilted delightfully, while a stubborn little chin showed she had no lack of character.

"First," French went on in low tones, glancing at the door, "I must tell you that I am a detective officer from Scotland Yard," and he handed her his official card.

He was accustomed to seeing apprehension appear in the faces of those to whom he made this announcement, both innocent and guilty, but he was not prepared for its effect upon Miss Moran. For a moment an expression of absolute terror twisted her features. Her eyes dilated and her face became a chalky white. Then with an obvious effort she murmured "Yes?"

"You were expecting a visit of this kind, were you not?" French went on. "You felt that sooner or later it must come?"

"Oh, no, no, no," she cried hoarsely, but with delightful suggestion of an Irish brogue. "Whatever do you mean?"

"I think you know. If you didn't, why should my visit terrify you?"

"I am not terrified," she declared in tremulous tones which belied her words. "Why should you think a thing like that anyway?"

"How can I think anything else, Miss Moran? There is no use in your taking that line. Your manner leaves no doubt of your feelings."

She made a determined effort to pull herself together.

"Well," she retorted with more confidence, "and can't you understand that the very appearance of a detective gentleman like yourself would be enough to frighten anyone."

French shook his head.

"It won't do, Miss Moran," he said, not unkindly. "You apprehend danger to yourself from my call. You cannot deny anything so obvious. But I want you to understand I'm not here to harm you. You have some information that I require. That is all."

116

She waited without speaking, evidently in no way reassured.

"First," went on French, still speaking in low tones, "my business is private. Are you sure we shall not be overheard? If there is any chance of that I shall ask you to come out with me and we can discuss the matter on a seat in one of the parks."

She nodded quickly. "That would be better," she agreed. "If you go on, I'll follow."

French rose. "Right, then. What about the Charing Cross Gardens near the Villiers Street entrance?" He remembered that this was where poor Thurza Darke had met Westinghouse.

To his delight the shot told. She gave him a quick, terrified glance as she faltered: "I'll be there in half an hour."

"Good." Then loudly for the benefit of anyone who might be listening. "Well, goodbye, Miss Moran. I'm glad to have had the pleasure of meeting you."

He had little doubt that the girl would keep her appointment, but he was not so sure that she would not first communicate with some member of the gang. Therefore, as soon as he was out of sight of the house in the direction she would expect him to take, he turned quickly down a side street, and by making a short detour, regained Nelson Street on the opposite side of the boarding house. Then stepping into a shop, he laid a shilling on the counter and asked if he might use the telephone.

"Scotland Yard speaking," he called softly. "Please keep a note of any calls from Gerrard 4763C during the next few minutes. Official demand to your headquarters following."

He had noticed the telephone in the hall of the boarding house. Luckily for him it was one of the old-fashioned instruments which bore a plate with the words "Your number is —" followed by the digits in question.

He left the shop quickly, so as to make sure that Miss Moran should not give him the slip. She had not appeared, and once more becoming an aimless lounger, he watched the boarding house door.

In about ten minutes she emerged and set off down the road. Slowly French followed. But she attempted no excursions aside and within a minute of the time appointed they met in the Gardens.

"Here is an empty seat," French said, when he had gravely complimented her on her punctuality. "Do you smoke?"

She accepted a cigarette, which he lit in silence, only continuing when she was comfortably settled.

"Now, Miss Moran, you mustn't be alarmed, but I have to tell you this is a serious matter that you've got mixed up in. And I may tell you too, that your only chance of keeping out of personal trouble is to be frank with me. If you tell me everything, I'll do my level best for you. But I assure you that I'm not threatening when I say that if you mislead me you'll bitterly regret it."

The girl had evidently been thinking during her walk, and she replied with some show of assurance.

"Och, sure, Mr French, I wouldn't dream of not being frank with you. But there's nothing I have to tell."

"I'm sorry to hear you say so," French returned, "because your face shows me the exact opposite. However, pass that for the moment. Will you tell me why you travel every morning for a few hundred yards in Mr Curtice Welland's car?"

The girl's white face paled still further, but she made no reply.

"Do take my advice, Miss Moran," French went on earnestly. "I may tell you in confidence it is not you that I want, but Welland. But if you persist in putting me off you'll be in the same trouble yourself. Believe me, you're playing a more dangerous game than you know."

For a few moments further she hesitated, then said sullenly:

"I'm not doing anything against the law."

"In that case, Miss Moran, you can't have any real objection to telling me all about it."

"You can't make me say a single word if I don't want to."

"Perfectly true. But I can arrest you on a charge of criminal conspiracy with Welland and certain other parties, and the public prosecutor will make you tell in open court at your trial."

"But you wouldn't do a thing like that?" She spoke half coaxingly, but the look of fear flashed again in her eyes.

"Not if you didn't force me to." French leant towards her and spoke very earnestly. "Don't you make any mistake, Miss Moran. It's my business to get this information and I'm going to get it. And what's more, you're going to give it me. You can please yourself whether you do it now or at Scotland Yard or at the Old Bailey. But you're going to give it to me." His voice became coaxing in its turn. "Why not now, just privately here between the two of us? I promise to help you and to protect you from your accomplices." He paused, then as she did not speak, went on: "Do be sensible, Miss Moran. You'll never get such a chance again. Remember, it would be a hundred times worse in open court with everyone against you."

French felt that he was sailing rather near the wind in speaking in this way. His justification to himself was that he was convinced of the girl's innocence, or rather that if guilty of crime, she had been terrorised into it and wished to escape. But he was not in a position to say this to her in so many words. He remained silent for a few minutes, then just as he was about to resume his arguments, she spoke, her emotion accentuating her brogue.

"I don't think that's a fair way you're speaking to me at all," she said in a low tone, "but how am I going to stand up against the whole British police? Sure I see that you've got me and I'll have to tell you what you want to know."

"Believe me, you won't regret it."

"Well, then, if you must know, it's about money," she began with a rush, as if, having decided to speak, she was now only anxious to get her recital over. "I've been hard up for money. And you'll be saying it's very wrong and foolish of me, but I've taken to gambling to raise the wind. That Mr Welland is a bookmaker. He has a scheme by which you can stake on the tables at Monte

Carlo, and you here in London all the time. A girl I met told me about it. That's what I'm doing in the car. Mr Welland said it was against the law to bet in the street and that his office was too far away, so he would lift me for a moment in his car while he took the money."

French could scarcely restrain a chuckle of sheer delight as he listened to this statement. It was even more gratifying news than that the girls with whom Welland was dealing were employed in box offices. For here was actual proof that he really was on the right track! The scheme for betting on the Monte Carlo tables connected the cases. When, therefore, he was investigating the affairs of Curtice Welland, he was on the way to learning who murdered Thurza Darke and her fellow victims. For the second time in two days he experienced that delightful feeling of enthusiasm which came from progress and success.

At the same time he was puzzled by the girl's manner. Experience told him that a true confession produced symptoms of relief. But Miss Moran had shown no such feeling. Indeed, she seemed more uneasy and apprehensive than ever. Gradually an opinion crystallised in French's mind. He had not heard the truth. This story was an invention and the girl was terrified lest he should see through it. A small test, however, should settle the matter.

"Betting may or may not be wise, Miss Moran," he said gravely, "but it is certainly not illegal and you have nothing to fear from the police because of it. There surely must be something else. Has your betting tempted you towards the till of the Panopticon?"

For a moment an indignant denial seemed imminent, then a fresh idea appeared to dawn on the girl's mind and she checked herself.

"Maybe there was something of the kind," she said, averting her face as if from shame. But French was certain she was now feeling relief.

So the little test had worked, and out of her own mouth the girl stood convicted. French's previous inquiries had proved that she was not stealing from the till. But she had seen that her story lacked motive and to bolster it up she had admitted a theft of which she was innocent.

The business, then, was even more serious than he had supposed. This girl was willing to risk arrest rather than reveal it. But French saw that for the moment he would get no more out of her, and he set himself to dispel her fears, so that the story she would almost certainly tell to Welland would do as little harm as possible.

One other point, however, he did learn. At that moment he did not appreciate its importance, but afterwards he saw that its discovery formed an essential link in the chain by which he eventually unravelled the mystery.

While going over with Miss Moran the places at which she had been picked up and set down, he remembered that she had not been seen to speak to Welland, and asked how she knew where to wait for the car. Without hesitation she told him that five different places had been chosen, which were used in rotation. This avoided stopping at the same place each day, which might be noticeable, and the number five insured a different place being used on the same day of each week.

"For example," she said, "today I'll be waiting for him at the corner of Old Compton Street and Greek Street and he'll run me to Green Street. That'll give me three or four minutes to fix up about the stakes. Tomorrow I start again where you saw me first, and so on."

From such slight threads are the webs of justice woven.

Before parting with her French became the heavy father. He told her he was satisfied that she was doing something which she would be wiser to leave alone, and though of course she was a free agent, he urged her for her own sake to give it up. At all events, if she found herself in any danger or difficulty she was to apply to the Yard, when he would see that she got the help she needed.

"And don't wait till it's too late," he concluded earnestly. "I don't want to frighten you, but I warn you very seriously to be careful. Keep this interview secret from Mr Welland. You may be in real personal danger if you don't. Other girls in your position have been indiscreet and have paid for it with their lives — I'm not exaggerating, Miss Moran — *with their lives*. So keep your mouth shut, and if you are in any danger don't hesitate to ring up the Yard — Victoria 7000."

She seemed considerably impressed as she gave him her promise. But she had kept her secret and French, despondent over his failure, told himself that his efforts had done nothing more than put the conspirators on their guard.

He wished her good day, and returned to the Yard. There he sent for no less than five men.

"Three of you men get yourselves up as taximen," he told them, "and take out cars. The other two and myself will be your passengers. You will stop in sight of the corner of Old Compton Street and Greek Street and watch for a grey saloon car lifting a girl. All of you follow this car. Drive as near it as possible and watch every motion that the girl makes. See if she speaks to the driver and if possible lip-read what she says. After she is set down in Green Street you are finished and can come back to the Yard."

This programme was carried out. When Molly Moran appeared at the end of Greek Street three cars were standing before offices in different parts of the street. On the appearance of Welland's car they started up their engines, and as he moved off they followed. One was slightly in front with its occupant watching out of the back window by means of a periscope, a second was almost abreast while the third ran on ahead to Charing Cross Road, ready to fall into place as Welland turned the corner.

French's three drivers showed immense skill in manœuvring their vehicles into places of vantage. During the whole period in which Miss Moran remained in the car, an observer was never more than ten feet away. Sometimes one of the three would be nearest, sometimes another, but none ever left the side of the grey car until the next was ready to take its place.

The result both pleased and puzzled French. It pleased him because it proved him correct in assuming the story of the gambling to be a fabrication. After a brief good morning, lip-read by Carter, the girl did not speak to Welland during the whole trip, nor did money or letters pass between them. But French was puzzled by what she did. For at least a minute she leant forward and appeared to feel at something at her feet.

He pondered over this for some time, but could think of no explanation but the obvious one that the girl was putting something into or taking something out of a hidden receptacle. If so, he must inspect the car and find it. Should this be his next step?

He thought so except for one point. Would it not be better to see first if he could get anything out of the other three girls?

Eventually he decided that it would. If his inquiries were reported to Welland it could scarcely matter whether it was by one girl or four. If he, French, knew as much as he evidently did know about the movements of Molly, Welland would recognise that he must know of the other girls also.

Next morning, therefore, he made three calls, in every case unfortunately without result. All the girls showed signs of anxiety, amounting almost to terror on learning his business. But all, after the application of a varying amount of pressure, told the story of the gambling. He was satisfied that each was lying and that the story had been rehearsed beforehand for use in just such an emergency.

There remained then the search of the car. To arrange an opportunity was not an easy proposition. For a time he considered means of getting it to the Yard, such as the arrest of Welland "by error," followed by an apology and an immediate release. But he thought that as long as any other way remained, his superiors would not stand for such a method. Besides, if by some remote chance the girls had not reported his activities to Welland, it would put the man on his guard.

At last he decided that there was nothing for it but for him once again to play the burglar. He must somehow get into the garage at night, when he would have plenty of time to make an exhaustive examination.

Though he did not see just how he was going to manage it, he decided that the very next day he would make the attempt.

CHAPTER
TEN

Mr Cracksman French

The first step which French took to meet his new problem was to make a reconnaissance of the enemy's country. He went early next morning to Tate's Lane, so as to get the job over before Welland should turn up. The gate of the coachbuilder's yard was open and he walked boldly in and had a look round.

A closer inspection confirmed the impression of a small, moribund business which the view from the street had suggested. The establishment covered a narrow frontage, but stretched a good way back. In the foreground stood a number of horse carts and lorries, awaiting the scrapheap, if one were to judge by appearances. These with some spare parts filled up all the open space to the high boundary wall on the left, except for a narrow passage to the back of the yard. Along the right ran a grimy brick building from which came the sound of hammering. The only structure with a well-to-do appearance was a new shed of about twenty feet by ten, built as a lean-to in the back left hand corner. Numerous pneumatic tyre tracks leading to the large door in the gable showed that this was Curtice Welland's garage.

Though the sounds from the shed indicated that work was there in progress, no one was to be seen in the yard. French therefore strolled close up to the garage to see if he could find a way to break and enter. But the more he saw the less easy this appeared. The building was of solid brickwork with a slated roof. The large door was fastened with the most modern form of chubb lock, against which French knew that his bent wires and skeleton keys would have but little chance. In the side wall was a small window with a fixed sash. The other two sides were formed by the unbroken boundary walls of the yard.

Thinking he had better not be seen poking about, he turned back to the shed and looked in. Three men were employed, one turning hubs at a small lathe, the other two assembling lorry bodies. On seeing French one of the latter came slowly forward. "Morning," said French. "You the boss?"

"'E's out," the man answered, adroitly expectorating. "'Oo want's 'im?"

"I do," French explained. "Name of Simkins. I want a garage for a car I've got and I was told that you let them."

The man shook his head.

"But I thought that garage in the corner was let to an outsider?"

"That's right. But the boss 'e didn't 'ave nothing to say to the building. 'E only let the ground."

"I follow you. Then it's occupied, is it? I couldn't get it, I suppose?"

"Not likely, you couldn't. The man wot keeps 'is car in that garage 'ad it specially built for 'im last year."

"Any chance of my getting a bit of ground to build another?"

"You'd 'ave to see the boss abaht that," the man declared. "I couldn't fix it for you."

"I want one like that in the corner," French persisted. "Could I see into it?"

"Not without you got leave from Mr Welland, you couldn't. 'E keeps the key. See 'ere, mister. You call back 'ere abaht three o'clock an' you'll see the boss. 'E'll tell you all you wants to know."

"That's common sense." French chatted pleasantly and a couple of shillings changed ownership. Then on his way to the gate he made a bid for the piece of information he required.

"I wonder you don't get your stuff stolen at night," he said, after leading up to the subject by remarks on the spare parts lying around. "But then I suppose you have a watchman?"

"We don't 'ave no watchman. It ain't necessary. It wouldn't be so easy for to steal anything as wot you'd think, mister. This is all 'eavyish stuff, and if anyone was to pass it out over the wall, ten chance to one but a bobby'd catch 'em on."

In a thoughtful mood French returned to the Yard. By hook or by crook he would examine that car, even if he had to commit a felony. He knew that if he were found out he would get into trouble, but he felt the case had dragged on so long that for his own reputation's sake he must get results without further delay.

On reaching the Yard he sent for Sergeant Ormsby. Ormsby had gone through his apprenticeship as a carpenter before he joined the force, and being skilful with his hands, he was in request where delicate manual work was required.

"I want to do a burglary tonight, Ormsby," French began. "Are you on to give me a hand? I can't tell you to, but I'd be glad of your help, and if there's trouble I'll stand the racket."

Ormsby grinned. "Right-ho, Mr French. It won't be the first time."

"I want to break into a garage. There's a heavy door with a chubb lock that we can't do nothing with. But there's a window that we might get the glass out of. The frame is glazed with a single pane of rough rolled, about eighteen inches by twenty-four."

"And you want me to take it out?"

"Right first shot. Can you do it, and put it back so's it won't be noticed?"

Ormsby shook his head. He could try, but he wouldn't go nap on the result.

"Then better take a pane with you."

"Are you sure of the size?"

"No, but take it big and take a diamond as well. You'll want the usual things, and some reddish brown paint and dust. We'll try and get the lock off from the inside and then perhaps you could cut a key."

Ormsby was dubious as to the possibilities, but delighted at the prospect of adventure, and departed jubilantly to get his paraphernalia together.

It was getting on towards two o'clock next morning when the two men set out. Both were wearing dark clothes, caps and rubber shoes. Except for Ormsby's pane of glass, wrapped up neatly in dark coloured paper, there was nothing to draw an observer's attention to them. In addition to the glass Ormsby had a small kit of tools, while French carried two electric torches and a large black overcoat.

Tate's Lane, when they reached it, was deserted save for a single policeman patrolling slowly towards its far end.

"When he goes round the corner we'll have our opportunity," said French, who had looked up the areas covered by all the adjacent beats.

They waited in York Street until the man disappeared, then followed him down Tate's Lane. Two minutes later they were at the coachbuilder's.

"Now for it," said French, glancing quickly round.

No one was in sight. Opposite, the houses were in darkness except for a single lighted window, which showed a dull yellow square against the surrounding gloom. Rather a nuisance, French thought. Someone over there was awake and might chance to look out.

"I'll go first," he whispered.

Ormsby laid his glass against the wall, and forming a back, gave French a hoist up on to the wall. A moment later French had dropped softly to the ground within. Quickly the glass and tools were handed over, and in ten seconds more Ormsby also was inside.

They stood listening, but the silence was reassuring, and they tiptoed to the garage and set to work on the window. French directed the beam from his torch and held up the coat to screen the light, while Ormsby tackled the removal of the glass.

The night was ideal for their purpose. There was no moon, but the light of the stars showed up faintly the larger objects, while allowing the men to work unseen. It was calm and sounds carried far. In the street they could hear the footsteps of the returning policeman ring sharply.

Soon the putty was cut away and the sprigs withdrawn. Then, affixing rubber suckers to the corners, Ormsby pulled. This was the critical operation, but he worked skilfully and gradually one corner after another came away and he was able to lift out the pane.

"Fine," French whispered. "Now a hand in."

A flash from the torch showed that there was a small bench beneath the window. With difficulty French squeezed through on to the bench and dropped noiselessly to the floor. Immediately he opened the door, Ormsby slipped in, and the door was shut.

Their first care was to rig the coat over the window lest the light should betray them. Then while Ormsby started on his door key, French with the other torch examined the car.

His search was extraordinarily thorough. From tyres to roof and from headlights to rear number-plate he went over every detail. But absolutely without result. The car was a perfectly normal 15/20 Mercury saloon, probably worth £450 when new. It was upholstered in grey leatherette and the small fittings were complete and excellent in quality.

With a helpless, baffled feeling, French stood pondering. Were all his ideas of the affair erroneous? Did these girls really use the car only to register bets with the driver?

For a moment he thought it must be so. Then the face of poor pretty Thurza Darke came up before his imagination as he had seen it in the Portsmouth police station. No. There was something in their drives more deadly and sinister than gambling. Crime, terrible and dastardly, lurked there.

Setting his jaw grimly, he turned back to the car. There *must* be something.

He sat down once more on the back seat, and stooping forward as the girls had done, marked the arcs which his fingers could reach. On that space he worked, examining joints, testing for secret springs, measuring cubic capacities. And then suddenly he found what he wanted.

Beneath the back seat was the petrol tank. This he had already measured and dipped, and it had seemed to fill the entire space. But now he found that a thin steel plate, hinged along the floor, turned up in front of the tank. It fitted so well that at first he had taken it for the front of the tank itself. But he had accidentally pressed a secret spring, and the plate had moved forward. Attached to the inside of the plate, and fitting into a recess in the tank, was a small steel pocket, lined with velvet. The recess was triangular in cross section, which explained the fact that he had been able to push Ormsby's steel rule right down to the bottom of the tank, and even feel round its edges, without discovering the trick.

French breathed a sigh of relief. At last the action of the girls was clear. On entering the car they had stooped down, lowered the plate, put in or taken out some object, raised the plate again and dismounted. After arrival from his round, or before starting, Welland had emptied or filled the pocket.

But beyond the admittedly crucial point that his suspicions had been proved justified, French had learned nothing. That the objects transmitted were small was now certain, but this had been probable from the first.

In vain he searched for some fragment in the velvet lining of the pocket which might indicate the nature of the transitory contents. In vain he longed for the skill of Dr Thorndyke, who might have been able with his vacuum extractor to secure microscopic dust from its fibres which would have solved the problem.

Satisfied that he had learnt all he could from the car, he turned to the examination of the building itself.

There was not much to examine. The four walls, unbroken save for door and window, were finished smoothly with cement. Under the window was the bench, a plain structure offering no hiding-place. The roof was not ceiled, the rafters, slating laths and slates being visible. The floor was of concrete, sloping slightly towards the central pit. A four-inch drain level with the bottom of the pit led away through the end wall opposite the door, and above it, let into the garage floor, was a cast-iron inspection chamber cover. A four-inch metal pipe rose up the wall and passed through the roof. All was perfectly normal and in order.

French glanced at his watch.

"Nearly finished, Ormsby?"

"Just about, Mr. French. See here."

He turned his new key in the lock and the bolt shot back.

"Good. We can get in now any time." French pointed to the pipe which ran up the wall. "What's that thing for?"

"Vent pipe," Ormsby returned. "That's all right. Required to ventilate the drain."

"I'm satisfied with everything here except the drains. Best have this inspection chamber cover off and see that all is O.K."

Beneath the cover the drain from the pit ran across the cement bottom in a channel, ending up in a drop or well full of water, above which was a round plug about four inches in diameter. Still higher up an open four-inch pipe led to the base of the vertical one.

"All perfectly O.K.," Ormsby pronounced. "Here is the drain from the pit leading into its disconnecting trap, and here," he pointed to the plug, "is the inlet for clearing out the pipe if it should get stopped. This," indicating the high-level open pipe, "is the vent pipe. It turns up the wall and has an outlet above the roof. All perfectly correct."

With a sigh French helped him to lift the inspection chamber cover into place. On the whole he was disappointed with his visit. He had hoped that it would have given him the solution of the mystery, but beyond proving that there really was a mystery, he had learnt nothing.

"Get that glass in," he said shortly.

Once again he held the torch and coat while Ormsby worked. Quickly the window was glazed and the fresh work painted with rapidly drying paint, which in its turn was dusted over with various coloured powders until it had practically resumed its original appearance. Then watching their chance, the two men climbed back into Tate's Lane and so to their respective homes.

The discovery of the secret pocket in the car seemed to French to rule out one of his theories. The scheme was not for the purpose of keeping members of an organisation in touch with headquarters. Something material was being handed over. What could it be?

The girls' occupation suggested money, some scheme for robbing the tills of their various establishments. But then, so far as his information went, they *weren't* robbing their tills.

There were two ways, French saw, to settle the matter. The first was to arrest two of the girls on some trumped-up charge, one just before she was picked up by the car, and the other immediately after she was set down. One or other would necessarily be carrying the stuff. The second way was to shadow Welland more closely than ever and take him in the act of receiving or parting with it.

Of the two, French preferred the second. To take the girls to the Yard on suspicion would precipitate events too rapidly. He would no doubt find out what was being passed as well as getting Welland, but Style and the girl Lestrange would probably give him the slip. And he must get all three, for all, he felt positive, were concerned in the murders. No, he was not yet ready to take action. He must first find out what was going on.

A more intense shadowing of Welland seemed therefore to be indicated. French went over in his mind what he had already learnt of the man's movements.

Observation had shown that on his journeys between his house, his office, his garage and the golf links he had held no communication with any other person. His entire time, therefore, was accounted for except the periods spent in those four places.

French called in two of his men and instructed them to get what help they required and watch the office and garage day and night, shadowing to his home anyone other than Welland who might enter either.

The house and links, he decided, he would tackle himself, and he settled down to think out a scheme for doing so.

CHAPTER
ELEVEN

The Happy Paterfamilias

Some fifteen minutes later he sent once more for Sergeant Ormsby.

"You have a son, haven't you, Ormsby?" he asked. "A nipper of about ten?"

"That's right, sir."

"A smart lad, able to put through a bit of play-acting?"

Ormsby smiled.

"If you had seen him doing Tom Mix in 'Miss Hook of Hollywood' at a children's show out our way you wouldn't need to ask."

"The very thing. Could you spare him for an hour or two tomorrow?"

"Of course, Mr French. He's on holidays now in any case."

"Then how would this work?" French outlined his plan and the other laughed.

"Suit the boy first-class," he observed with a chuckle, "and suit me too for the matter of that."

"Good, then we'll leave in time to be at Harrow Station before the 9.17 in the morning."

Next day French and an intelligent but somewhat mischievous looking boy alighted at Harrow shortly before nine. They were dressed for their parts. French was obviously a landed proprietor on a visit to town, while Freddy Ormsby was a convincing study of a preparatory schoolboy. Having seen Welland leave by the 9.17, they strolled into the town.

"Now, sonny, we've got to kill an hour or two. What would you like? Coffee or an ice?"

Freddie's predilection being for ices, they found a shop and gave a bumper order. French sipped coffee and smoked a lengthy pipe, and then they went for a walk. It was not till nearly eleven that they found themselves at the end of Acacia Avenue.

"Now, Fred, here we are. Do your best, like a good chap."

They strolled down the road, evidently strangers to the place, and as evidently father and son. At all vacant lots they stopped, clearly discussing a possible dwelling. Next door to No. 39 was such a lot, and at this they halted in its turn.

"That bow window on the ground floor," French said in low tones, as he demonstrated with gestures how the ground might be terraced.

On his previous visit he had noted the exterior of the house, and by plotting the various elevations, he had deduced its probable plan. From this he was satisfied that the window in question belonged to Welland's sitting-room. No other had a large enough expanse of blank wall beside it for the necessary size of the room.

Freddie Ormsby acted with promptitude.

"Oh, daddy, see!" he cried in shrill tones. "Look where the cat is!" and before his scandalised parent could intervene, he had picked up a stone and sent it whizzing with unerring aim through the largest pane.

"Played, sir! Fine shot!" French whispered, then in loud tones: "Well, upon my soul, you little rascal! Look what you've done. What do you mean, sir, by such conduct?"

The door of No. 39 was opened by an elderly woman with an indignant countenance as an angry but apologetic gentleman and a scared, woebegone boy approached up its tiny drive.

"I'm afraid, madam," said French, taking off his hat politely, "that an accident has occurred for which I am responsible. My son has so far forgotten himself as to throw a stone which unfortunately has broken your window. He had been warned about stone-throwing again and again, and I'll see that this time it will be a lesson to him. I can only offer you, madam, my apologies, and go at once for a glazier to make good the damage."

The good lady, who had evidently been prepared to breathe threatenings and slaughter, on finding the wind thus taken out of her sails, became somewhat mollified.

"Oh, well, if that's the way you put it, it will be all right," she admitted, "though it did give me a start and no mistake, the stone coming through. But there," she went on magnanimously, glancing at the frightened culprit, "you don't need to say too much to 'im. Boys will be boys, that's what I say. Boys will be boys."

"It's excessively kind of you to look at it like that," French declared. "As I said, I can assure you it will be a lesson to him he will not forget. I hope nothing has been damaged inside the room?"

"Well, I 'aven't looked yet. Better come in and see for yourself."

"Thank you. And I think it will save time if I get a sample of the glass and measure the window."

Having adjured "Cecil" to wait for him and not to get into any more mischief while his back was turned, French followed the housekeeper. The room, as he had imagined, was Welland's sitting-room. It was comfortably though not luxuriously furnished. In the window was a deep saddlebag armchair with beside it a table bearing some papers. Against one wall was a roll-top desk, with the cover down. A tantalus and a cigar cabinet stood on a second table. Many shelves of books hung on the wall.

"The desk," thought French, as he expressed his relief that no further damage had been done and took his measurements. Two minutes later he withdrew in an atmosphere of politeness and regrets.

"You did that well, old man," he congratulated his now grinning companion, when at last they were clear of Acacia Avenue. "You shall have five bob and the best lunch I can get you."

At the station they met Ormsby, clad in a glazier's well-worn overalls and with smudges of paint on his cap.

"He did it fine," French greeted him, "you'll be having the lad on the films yet. There's the size of the pane and there's what it was glazed with. Have you got what'll do it?"

"No," said Ormsby, "but there's a glazier's down the street. I'll get it there. It was the room you wanted all right?"

"Yes, and there's a desk in it that you'll have to go through. How'll you do if the old woman sticks in the room?"

Ormsby smiled. "Trust me for that, Mr French. You may not have known it, but it sometimes takes a terrible lot of hot water to glaze a pane. I'll keep her boiling up fresh kettles."

Three hours later Ormsby knocked at the door of French's room at the Yard.

"There's absolutely nothing there, Mr French," he began, as he took the seat to which the other pointed. "I had a bit of luck, and I've been through practically the whole house and there's not a thing that you could get hold of. In the first place that woman's a bit deaf and that helped me."

"I noticed it," said French.

"Yes. Well, I went to the door and said I was the man come to glaze the pane and she had me in at once and I got to work. She hung about for a minute or two, but I didn't speak, and when she saw me getting at it, she said she would be next door in the kitchen if I wanted anything and went out."

"Lucky for you."

"Wasn't it, sir? But better than that, she was washing clothes and as long as I could hear the suds going I knew I was safe. I made some mess round the window to show I was working and then I went for the desk. It was an easy lock and I had it open in twenty seconds. I went through everything and there's not a paper nor any other thing that shouldn't be there. All absolutely O.K."

"Pity," French interjected.

"Isn't it? Then I made some more mess and had a look round the room and a quick run through the books. Then the old lady came in to see how I was getting on."

He paused, and French nodded his appreciation of the situation.

"She seemed satisfied with the amount of the mess and went back to the kitchen without speaking and I heard the washing start again. I thought I might take a bit of risk, so I slipped upstairs and found the man's bedroom. I was afraid to stay too long, but I was long enough to make sure there was nothing there either. So then I came down and finished up the pane and painted the putty and came away."

"Well, that's that, Ormsby."

"Sorry I couldn't get more, Mr French."

"We may do our best to cook evidence," French said, with the twinkle in his eye showing even more clearly than usual, "but I draw the line at inventing it if it's not there."

Here was another disappointment. French had been building more even than he knew on Ormsby's search of the house, and when this also had drawn blank, his chagrin was correspondingly great. The affair was certainly exasperating. It was a long time since he had felt so completely puzzled.

There was nothing for it, however, but to carry on with the plan he had made, and five o'clock that afternoon saw him at the clubhouse of Welland's golf course, inquiring for the secretary.

"This is a confidential matter, Mr Allan," he began when he was seated in that gentleman's office, "and I do not know that I can claim your help in it. I can, however, ask for it, and that I am going to do."

The secretary murmured politely.

"It concerns a member of your club," went on French, "Mr Curtice Welland. Now I may say in confidence that we have reason to suspect that Mr Welland may not be all that he appears to be. In fact we think," French dropped his voice, "that he is one of a trio involved in no less a crime than murder."

The secretary stared.

"Curtice Welland?" he repeated incredulously. "Surely not, Inspector. Curtice Welland involved in a murder! You can't ask me to believe that." He shook his head decisively.

"Then you know him well?"

"As a matter of fact, I don't. I really scarcely know him at all. But he has always seemed so quiet and inoffensive; the last type of man that one would associate with such a crime."

"So was Dr Crippen, and so was many another murderer, Mr Allan," French said seriously. "Manner and appearance are unfortunately no guide, as you would know if you had my experience. But I make no accusation against the man. It may be that the Yard is mistaken in its view. And that's what I have been sent here to find out. I am investigating Mr Welland's life and character. And it is in that capacity I have come to ask your help."

Allan hesitated, frowning.

"Mr Welland is a member of the club," he said at last. "He is in a sense my employer. I don't know that I feel at liberty to discuss him even if I knew anything against him, which thank heaven I don't."

"Well, sir," said French with a smile, "if you don't know anything, that settles the matter, doesn't it?" Then he came to his real objective. "But there is a bit of quite harmless information that perhaps you could give me. It is a list of Mr Welland's particular friends among the members or of any with whom he plays regularly. This will not be giving anything away on your part, because you must see that I could find it out for myself by simple observation."

Allan replied with evident relief. He would be glad to help the inspector, but there were no such persons. Welland had catholic tastes. He played with anyone who was available, not with anyone in particular.

French was more than ever worried as he returned to the Yard. Almost in despair he redoubled his efforts. He put a number of men on to watch Welland's house, others he had shadow him while golfing and at other free times, but all without avail. As the days passed and he found that no one visited the garage or the office, and that Welland came into no regular touch with any human being other than the four girls, he became almost ill from anxiety. Gone was his usual cheery optimism, his suavity, his pleasant words for his subordinates. "Soapy Joe" was soapy no longer.

And then quite suddenly, as he lay one night racking his brains over the problem, an explanation of the whole business shot into his mind. Tremulously he considered the idea, and the more he thought over it the more certain he grew that he was right.

Material objects were being carried in the secret pocket of the car. Material objects were being put in by Welland and taken out by the girls, and cash was being put in by the girls and taken out by Welland. The affair was a commercial proposition of a highly lucrative, but highly immoral and illegal type. These people were selling prohibited drugs!

And a good scheme it certainly was! Welland in some way as yet unknown was getting the "snow" or other stuff in bulk and making it up into small packages. Every morning he would start out with four bundles of such packages in the pocket of his car. Every day each girl would remove a bundle and replace it with a roll of notes. Every night, on some preconcerted signal from her customer, she would pass out with the metal disc of entrance to the cinema a package of the stuff, pocketing the notes given in exchange. The illicit sale of drugs had increased by leaps and bounds, and of all the methods of which French had yet heard, this was certainly the best.

Here was ample motive for murder! Let the gang get wind of communication between any of their victims and Scotland Yard and the victim's fate was sealed.

Both the gains of success and the penalties of failure were too great to permit of any risks being run.

In a few moments French's whole outlook on life had changed. Gone was his weariness, his lassitude, his depression. Once more he was the optimist, about to add one more laurel to the many he had achieved in his career.

For this case would make a sensation. If there was one thing more than another which the authorities were keen on suppressing, it was this drug traffic. If he pulled off a big coup in this line, it could not fail to affect his prospects.

And then came the usual reaction. It was not all so clear as he had imagined. How and from whom was Welland getting the stuff? How and to whom was he passing on the money? French saw that he had a good way to go before his case should be complete.

As he thought of this side of the affair he swore from vexation. Why, every investigation that he had made had tended to show that the man was neither obtaining drugs in bulk nor disposing of large sums of money! Curse it all! he thought, was there ever such a tangle?

Almost in despair he had just decided that he would have to fall back on his alternative scheme and arrest and search two of the girls, when a further possibility occurred to him. Could he not keep so close a watch on the girls while in their box offices that he could not fail to see small packages being passed out?

To think of the idea was to act on it. Early next morning French was once again closeted with the manager of the Panopticon, in confidence putting forward his suspicions and begging the other's help towards testing them.

As a result of their deliberations, three men in the garb of electrical fitters arrived an hour later at the cinema. The boss of the little gang was named Ormsby, and his helpers Carter and Harvey. It seemed that an electric main in the corner of the entrance hall had given indications of fusing and immediate repairs had become necessary.

The defect, it appeared, was hidden in the wooden panelling alongside the box office presided over by Molly Moran, and the first job of the fitters was naturally to protect their work from passers-by. When, therefore, the staff came on duty for the afternoon session, they found that a neat canvas structure had been erected beside the box office. Behind this the men worked, and from this at five o'clock they went home.

All but one. From twelve-thirty that morning till eleven-thirty that night French sat behind the screen, his eyes glued to a hole in the canvas. From this he could see every movement of Molly's hands on the little desk some five feet away.

His view, of course, was limited. His peep-hole was but slightly in front of the office and the side wall of the opening cut off all movement on the back of the little counter. But he could not have placed his observation point further forward, as his sight would then have been impeded by the backs of the purchasers. But over a small area he had a perfect view, and he did not believe that anything could be slipped across unobserved by him.

The watch was tedious, but not so tedious as if he had had to be on the strain all the time. He knew that no attempt such as he expected could be made during periods of rush booking: it would be too dangerous. It was, therefore, only the booking of isolated persons that he had to watch. And there were other alleviations. The noise outside was so great that he was able to change his position without fear of discovery. Moreover, he had taken in a goodly supply of food, which he consumed at frequent intervals. But still he thought the time would never come to an end. Stiff and sore and with a splitting headache he waited, until at last after the performance, when all but the manager had left, he crept out and thankfully stretched his cramped limbs.

His physical discomfort was, however, as nothing to his mental perturbation. For he had seen nothing! Moreover, so good had been his outlook, that he was satisfied that there had been nothing to see. Nothing was being passed out with the entrance checks. Of that he could swear.

His drug theory was therefore false. Whatever Welland was doing, it was not peddling opium. Something else was being transferred through the medium of the secret panel in the car.

French could have wept when he found himself forced to this conclusion. Never in his life had he been up against anything which had puzzled him more. He would give a month's pay, he thought savagely, to get the thing cleared up.

That evening he had recourse once more to his household oracle. Again he put his difficulties before

Mrs French, and again light seemed to come from doing so. Not that this time she made any suggestions. Rather it was that his own mind clarified and he saw that there was only one thing left for him to do.

The arrest of the girls would be too dangerous. He must therefore get Molly Moran's confidence. By hook or by crook he must force her to tell her true story. And if he couldn't frighten or cajole her into keeping his interference secret from Welland, why then he must just take the consequences. He determined he would see her again, first thing next day.

CHAPTER
TWELVE

The Car's Freight

At nine o'clock next morning French rang up the number he had noted on the Nelson Street boarding house telephone, and asked for Miss Molly Moran.

"It's in connection with our previous conversation, Miss Moran," he explained. "There is a fresh development which I want to discuss with you. Will you meet me in half an hour at the same place as before?"

Though she agreed, French could sense the unwillingness in her tones. "Very good of you," he declared. "I'll not keep you long."

He greeted her pleasantly when she appeared, led the way to a deserted seat in the Charing Cross Gardens, supplied her with a cigarette, and for a few moments chatted of everyday matters. Then when she seemed more at her ease he turned to business.

"What I want to see you about is this, Miss Moran," he said more gravely. "Since our last interview I have learnt that this matter of Mr Welland is even more serious than I thought. I want to tell you what I know and to ask your further help. And first, are you quite satisfied that I really am from Scotland Yard? Would you like to go with me to the Yard where I am known?"

"Oh, no, Mr French," she answered hastily, "that's not necessary at all. I am perfectly satisfied."

"Very good. Now I told you before that I believed you were in personal danger from your association with this man. I want to tell you why I think so."

She did not reply, but sat with a bored expression, evidently trying to conceal her interest.

"Nearly three months ago," went on French, "a young lady named Thurza Darke was sent to the Yard by a solicitor. This man had found out that she had got into the clutches of a gang of crooks, and he sent her to us for protection. Now, Miss Moran, this young lady was employed in the box office of the Milan Cinema in Oxford Street. That is the first point.

"She said that on her way to business she had met a young lady in the train, a Miss Gwen Lestrange. She was a wealthy young lady, or seemed to be, and they got talking about her money. As Miss Lestrange said she was only a barmaid in a theatre, Miss Darke asked where it came from. With some appearance of hesitation she was told it was from gambling at second hand on the Monte Carlo tables. After further conversation Miss Lestrange suggested that Miss Darke should have a fling in the same way, and agreed to introduce her to the man with whom she herself dealt. He was then called Westinghouse. They met here in this garden, and Westinghouse arranged the gambling."

There was no question now of Miss Moran's attention. She was watching French with tense interest, in fact with an expression almost of horror.

He glanced at her with satisfaction.

"Is there any need for me to go on, Miss Moran?" he said gently. "Can you not imagine the rest? How Miss Darke won fair sums at first and thought she was going to make her fortune. Then how she began to lose; how at last she got into debt to Westinghouse; how he became threatening and swore he would report her to the cinema authorities; how he threatened prosecution, imprisonment, until the poor girl was almost beside herself with terror. You can picture it, can you not, Miss Moran?"

That she could picture it in vivid detail was evident. Her eyes were dilating and her face had paled.

"The remainder you can imagine also," went on French. "How at this crisis Miss Lestrange turned up unexpectedly; how she was sympathetically concerned about Miss Darke's woebegone appearance, and how she recommended recourse to her cousin, who, she said, had helped her out of a similar difficulty. Then how this man played on Miss Darke's fears in order to entrap her in his evil schemes. Ah, I see I needn't go into it further. You evidently know as much as I do about it."

In truth the girl's appearance left no doubt on the point. French, pausing for a moment, continued:

"Now I must tell you something that had happened earlier. A very great friend of Miss Darke's, a young lady also employed in the box office of a cinema, had recently died. She was a jolly, gay young thing, but for several weeks she had appeared to be in trouble. Then one day she disappeared, and later her body was found in a pool in a quarry. There was a verdict of suicide, but

Miss Darke never believed she had committed suicide. She said she was not that kind of girl, and she was convinced that she had been murdered.

"Now Miss Darke had tried to get out of her friend the cause of her trouble, but beyond the fact that it was due to some man who had got her into his power, the girl would not say. But she had described the man, and what had terrified Miss Darke was that the man to whom Miss Lestrange had sent her exactly answered the description.

"This was his description: middling tall, thinnish, fair-haired, rather terrifying eyes, and" — French paused for a moment, then added — "a purple scar shaped like a sickle on the inside of his left wrist."

Miss Moran gave a little gasping cry. She had gone dead white and swayed as if faint.

"Steady on, Miss Moran," French said sharply, but in low tones. "You don't want to attract attention. You're all right and perfectly safe. Pull yourself together."

With an evident effort the girl did so. She did not belie the evidence of her firm little chin. Again French told himself she was a young woman of character.

"You mustn't be alarmed," he went on. "I'm here to help you out of your difficulties. We'll discuss that in a moment. Meanwhile I must finish my story.

"As I say, Miss Darke recognised the man, and very wisely she temporised. If he would give her a couple of days to think it over she would come to a decision. He agreed. By friends about whom I needn't explain, she was persuaded to report the circumstances at the Yard.

Miss Moran," French's voice became very grave, "she was evidently watched. That night she disappeared, and two days later her body was found in the sea near Portsmouth. In this case there was no question of suicide. The poor girl had been murdered before being thrown into the sea."

Once again his listener's pallor grew deathlike, and once again with an evident effort she pulled herself together.

"I have one other thing to tell you. Inquiries revealed the fact that some five months before Miss Darke's friend's murder, another young lady was found drowned under suspicious circumstances. She also was in the box office of a cinema. Absolute proof was not obtainable, but there is no reasonable doubt that she also was murdered by the same gang."

French paused, carefully lit a cigarette, glanced keenly around and resumed.

"From all this, Miss Moran, you will see that when I said I thought you might be in personal danger, I was basing my opinion on something very real. I do not wish to frighten you unduly, but you must see that unless some steps are taken it may be your turn next. Now the question is: Are you going to be wise and confide in me?"

She did not answer and French also smoked in silence to let the question sink into her mind. Presently he went on: "There is also another side of the affair which you must not overlook and about which it is only fair that I should warn you. We now know so much about what is going on that it is only a question of time before we learn it all. If you are then found to be doing something illegal you will undoubtedly be charged with conspiracy in the crime. If on the other hand, you do all you can to help the authorities, I will do all I can to help you. Even if the matter should be too serious for me to keep you out of court, your having turned King's evidence would get you off."

It was evident that this view had not occurred to the young lady. She looked even more frightened and unhappy, though still she did not speak.

French grew impatient.

"Very well," he said in sharper tones, "I warn you again that your own safety requires that you should tell what you know, but if you won't take my warning I can't help it. I am of opinion that here and now you are carrying with you the object or objects which you will shortly place in the secret panel of Mr Welland's car. I shall have to take you into custody on a charge of conspiracy and have you searched so as to find out what that article is."

His conscience pricked him slightly as he spoke. Was this strictly in accordance with the rules for the interrogation of a possible witness? Then he thought he was justified. This girl would not incriminate herself. He could swear she was innocent. And anything was good enough for the murderers of Thurza Darke.

The girl gave a little cry.

"Take me into custody!" she whispered hoarsely. "Surely you wouldn't do a thing like that?"

"I certainly would. I am going to find out about this business at whatever cost. Come now," he went on more coaxingly, "be wise and come in on the side that must win. As you are, you are running a terrible risk."

Though he spoke gravely, with secret delight he noticed signs of breaking down. Miss Moran shivered and slow, long sobs shook her frame. He remained silent and then at last he heard what he had been hoping for.

"Oh," she cried piteously, "but this is terrible altogether! I never thought anything like this would happen to me. I didn't mean any harm and now look at the trouble I'm in. You'll make it as easy as you can for me if I tell you?"

"I have already promised, Miss Moran. Not only that, but you'll feel a weight off your mind. You can't have been happy with this going on."

"Happy! I've been miserable. God only knows how miserable I've been. And if I have been making money, sure I've paid for it by the terror I've been in. I'll tell you everything."

She was sobbing freely and French once more urged her to control herself lest attention should be drawn to her. Presently in rather tremulous tones she began.

"The whole thing happened just as you say, Mr French. Every day I go to business by the tube and it was there I met the girl you spoke of. We got to be the best of friends, but all the time I was wondering where she got her money. One day I asked her, and she told me about the betting at Monte Carlo. She said if I would like a go at it she would arrange it for me, all just as you said. She said the bookmaker would meet us here. He did and he was the very man you described.

Och, but he was a terrible man, Mr French! There was something about his eyes that would give you the cold shivers. He was the man you mentioned anyway, for I saw the scar on his wrist."

"Ah," said French with satisfaction. "Did he tell you his name?"

"He did. It was Style."

"Good! That's the man. And did you stake?"

"I did, and I won first and then I lost. At that time Gwen Lestrange had got a job out of London and had gone away, but I met her by chance and she asked me how I was getting on. When I told her she said she thought her cousin could help me and she introduced me to him. That was Mr Welland."

French was highly pleased. At last he was making progress. Welland and Style had been concerned in the death of Thurza Darke, and already he had Welland under observation. A little more of that observation would undoubtedly lead him to Style.

He wondered why the two scoundrels had changed their respective roles. In Thurza Darke's case, Welland (or Westinghouse) had been the bookmaker and Style the cousin. In Molly Moran's, Style was the bookmaker and Welland the cousin. Probably, thought French, to divide equally both the risks and the responsibilities. With some surprise he also noted that while Welland had taken the precaution to change his name, Style had not troubled to do so. No doubt for this also there was a reason.

"Well, and what did Mr Welland say to you?"

The girl was evidently trying hard for self-control. She succeeded in choking down her sobs, but her voice was still tremulous as she went on.

"He was as pleasant and friendly as you'd wish. He said he was sorry about my difficulties and that he could offer me a job which would not only get me out of them, but would pay me well besides. And it wouldn't interfere with my work at the cinema, for all he wanted could be done between times when I wasn't selling tickets. He said it was the fine easy job, but it had one thing about it that I mightn't like, and then he looked at me and asked me was I very straightlaced in my ideas.

"Well, as a matter of fact, Mr French, I'm not straightlaced at all. So I said not, and he said that was fortunate, as it was the only drawback the job had. There were some straightlaced people who might object to it, but not ordinary men and women of the world. Anyway it was safe enough and absolutely moral and no one would ever know anything about it. Besides, I needn't go on with it unless I wanted to.

"I asked him what the job was and he said that was going too fast, he would have to have my word first to carry it out for at least a week. After that I could go on or not, as I liked. He said that if I promised, he would begin by giving me enough to square Mr Style. Then he said that maybe I would like a day or two to think it over and that I could come back and see him again."

"A plausible ruffian," French commented, now speaking in his pleasantest tones. "I'm sure that's just what he said to your predecessors. And what did you answer?"

The girl hung her head.

"Well, Mr French, I'm not pretending I didn't do wrong, but just think of my position. I had only my job to live by and I was going to lose it in a way that would have prevented me getting another. Then there was this job offered me, maybe not just all right, but safe anyway. It was a choice of two evils; of possible ruin if I accepted or of certain ruin if I didn't. I took the chance."

"Of course you did. I can see the fix you were in and I'm not blaming you."

"Well, to make a long story short, I told Mr Welland I would take his job. He smiled and shook hands and congratulated me. He said I'd never be sorry for what I was doing and then he handed me ten pounds, saying that here was part of the money I owed Mr Style and that if I paid this much, Mr Style would certainly give me time to meet the rest. He made me sign an I.O.U. for it, and he said I had better go and pay Mr Style at once.

"Next time Mr Style came to the Gardens I was waiting for him. He was very threatening at first, but when I showed him the ten pounds it changed his manner. He said he was glad I wasn't going to make trouble and that he would take that on account and give me three more weeks to find the other fifteen. He was so pleasant that in spite of the job I felt easier in my mind than I had for many a day."

"I don't wonder," French commented. "I think you did what any other girl would have done in your position, though I suppose I should not say so."

"Mr Welland had given me an appointment for two hours later and I met him in Hyde Park. He told me that one of his friends was in the Mint and had unexpectedly found a crate full of old half-crowns in a disused cellar. He supposed they had been called in for renewal and been forgotten. The friend did not see why they should lie there, and he began taking some home every evening. But he was afraid to get rid of them, for some of them bore the Mint rejection mark. He had consulted Mr Welland as to how this might be done, and that was where I came in. My job would be to pass out the half-crowns to the public. Every morning Mr Welland would give me so many and I was to pay them out in change at the paybox. For every half-crown I paid out I was to put another aside from the till for Mr Welland, and when I met him next day I was to hand these over to him, less a percentage."

"And did you believe his story?"

The girl hung her head.

"No," she admitted in a low voice, "but as he put it, it didn't seem so bad. He said the whole business, so far as I was concerned, was perfectly honest. The half-crowns were good and worth their full value. My cash at the cinema could be examined at any moment and would be found O.K. The only thing the most straitlaced could object to was his friend's taking these old coins from the Mint in the first instance. But I had nothing to do with that."

"And once again, did you believe that?"

"No," and the girl's voice was very mournful, "and I said I didn't to Mr Welland. But it was no good. He said that if I felt the slightest qualms about the matter, not to go on with it on any account at all. He would be the last person to press me to do what I thought wrong. I had only to hand him back his ten pounds and I would be clear of it."

"He had you there."

"He had me so that I couldn't wriggle. I begged him to let me go, but he said ten pounds were ten pounds, and that he couldn't afford to lose all that money and get nothing against it. Then I said I would tell the police the whole thing. That annoyed him. He advised me just to try it. He asked me did I imagine my story would be believed? There was I without a scrap of proof, but he had my I.O.U. He said if I went to the police it would be me that would go to prison for perjury and defamation of character."

"So you agreed to pass the money?"

"What else could I do, Mr French? I owed fifteen pounds to one of these men and ten to the other, and both said they would get me the sack if I didn't pay. And I hadn't any money and they wouldn't give me time."

Here, thought French in high delight, was something tangible at last! A gleam of light was beginning to illumine these mysterious happenings. With keener interest he went on.

"You said less a percentage?"

"Yes, ten per cent. One half-crown in every ten they let me keep."

"And how many do you change per day?"

"Well, of course it varies, but it would be a bad day that I wouldn't change a hundred. The most I ever did was a hundred and forty-five."

"Bless my soul, you've not been doing so badly! What have you been making? Eight or ten pounds a week?"

"About that. As I say, it varies, but I generally get at least eight."

French was astonished. No wonder this gang secured loyal helpers! With her ordinary wages this girl must be in receipt of something not far short of six hundred a year. He had certainly frightened her to some purpose if she was willing to risk the loss of such an income.

"H'm," he said with grim pleasantry. "It really looks like a case of your money or your life. But I don't want to keep you here too long. From what you tell me it would be better that we shouldn't be seen together. Just explain how you carry the half-crowns to and from the cinema."

"In my vanity bag." She was about to open it, but French checked her.

"Don't show me," he said. "Explain."

"There are three compartments in this bag. The centre one is like an ordinary bag, and I keep my own things in it, handkerchief and so on. The two side ones shut with a spring, and unless you examined the bag very carefully, you wouldn't know they were there. One of these spring compartments is coloured red inside and the other green. In the red one are the half-crowns from Mr Welland. As I take them out I put other half-crowns from the till into the green one. Sometimes I don't get all Mr Welland's changed, and the colours keep them separate."

"Why do you only put in half-crowns? Wouldn't two shillings and a sixpence from the till do as well?"

"I don't know. Mr Welland told me to put in half-crowns only."

Evidently to keep the percentage of coins of various values normal in the till, French imagined. If so, it showed an attention to detail which deserved success. He thought rapidly whether he had got all the information he could expect from this particular source, and decided that he had.

"Now, Miss Moran," he said earnestly, "you must be careful of yourself for a few days. Go straight home after your show and keep to populous streets. Even in the daytime avoid lonely places. Don't accept a message from anyone you don't know. Most important of all, don't get into any kind of a private car or taxi. This is not to frighten you, but to keep you safe. A few days and we'll have the gang and then you will be all right. One thing: if you notice anything in the least degree suspicious, ring me up — Victoria 7000. You will find plenty of help if you're in trouble. You understand all that?"

"Oh, yes, Mr French. And I can't say how glad I am to have told you. I was making money all right, but no money would be worth the terror I've endured. Mr Welland was always telling me that if the thing leaked out I was done for. It would be the sack for certain and maybe prison as well. I've been perfectly wretched and the relief is just beyond words."

French nodded gravely as the girl finished speaking. Another explanation of the affair had just flashed into his mind, an explanation so obvious that he could not understand why he had not instantly thought of it. *These coins had never seen the Mint!* They were forgeries. He would have staked long odds that he was on to a gang of (counterfeit) coiners.

If so, he must get hold of some samples without delay.

"What have you got in your bag now?" he asked. "Coins from Mr Welland or from the till?"

"From the till. These are the coins I changed yesterday. I'll find Mr Welland's parcel in the car in an hour's time."

"Of course. I should have known that. Now, I'll see you again at the Panopticon. You'll be sent for by the manager. Take your bag with you. Do you see?"

"Very good, Mr French. I'll remember all you have told me."

"Well, my last word to you is three don'ts: don't be frightened, don't let Mr Welland suspect our meeting, and don't do anything rash," and wishing her a pleasant good afternoon, he strolled out of the Gardens.

CHAPTER
THIRTEEN

The Transport of Supplies

Inspector French continued his stroll along the Embankment until he reached the Yard. There, after an interview with his chief, he got a cheque for ten pounds, and going to the nearest bank, asked for the money to be paid in half-crowns. With his pockets weighted down with the silver he went on to the Panopticon and asked for the manager. As a result of his conversation he was shown into a waiting room, where presently he was joined by Molly Moran.

"You here already, Mr French?" she greeted him.

"Yes. I want to get hold of some of those coins. Here is ten pounds worth of half-crowns. Just count me out eighty of Mr Welland's."

"But there's nothing remarkable about them at all. They're just ordinary half-crowns. I've shown them to a friend of mine in a bank, and he said so too."

"Oh," said French, "so a bank clerk has seen them, has he? But were you not afraid to tell him about them?"

"I didn't tell him at all. What I thought was that maybe they weren't good, that maybe Mr Welland's friend was making them — counterfeit coining, don't you call it? So I showed my friend four and said they had been refused on the grounds that they weren't good. He said they were perfectly all right."

"Oh," French repeated more dubiously. "Well, I'll have the eighty all the same. You might let me see that bag now that we can't be overlooked."

It was just what Miss Moran had described, a plain but large vanity bag with a central compartment of normal appearance, and two side ones, each capable of carrying some hundred and fifty half-crowns and fitted with an inside skin or bag which could be lifted out with the coins. When these side compartments were closed by their spring latches they were invisible to casual inspection, though if the bag were handled their existence became obvious. French was not surprised therefore to learn that Welland had given the strictest instructions that the bag was to be carried looped on the girl's arm, and never taken off except when she was actually working in the paybox.

But his interest in the bag was but slight compared with that he felt in the coins which Miss Moran had received from Welland. There were 130 and he tumbled them out on a table and began to turn them over.

His first glance surprised him and increased that feeling of depression which the girl's story of the bank clerk had aroused. That they were not new was undoubted; all had clearly been in circulation. Moreover the dates varied, and roughly speaking, the wear on any individual coin corresponded with its age.

Welland's story was unlikely enough at the best, but here already was proof of its falsity. These coins had not been recalled from circulation because of age or wear. They were still perfectly good.

French swore internally as he realised the conclusion to which he was being forced. If these coins were of different dates and had been in circulation, they were not forgeries. Dies were expensive and difficult to make and it was beyond belief that a series with different dates should have been obtained. Again, once the coins had been got into circulation, the counterfeiters would have finished with them. They would not be trying to get rid of them now.

He set himself to re-examine the samples with greater care. And the more he did so, the more convinced of their genuineness he became. So far as his lens revealed the design, the detail seemed perfect, the colour, feel and texture were normal, and every coin which he tested gave a satisfactory ring. He would, of course, have them examined by the experts at the Mint, but he had little doubt his own conclusion would be confirmed.

If so, it seemed to follow that the coins had been stolen. But he could not think of any source from which they might have been obtained. It was absurd to suppose they had been taken from the Mint. Coins of such an age and in such a condition would not be there. Nor did it seem likely that a bank had been robbed. Such an operation would be extremely difficult, and further, if it had been found possible, it was difficult to see why half-crowns alone had been taken. The only explanation which French could devise was that some eccentrically-minded miser had spent his

168

life hoarding them. But if so, and Welland had stolen them, why should he hesitate to pay them out himself?

On this latter point, however, a little further thought supplied an explanation. The one feature of the affair which was clear beyond doubt was that it was being carried out on a very large scale. If Miss Moran changed eight hundred half-crowns a week, it was to be presumed that each of the other girls did the same. Say, three thousand half-crowns a week — 150,000 a year! Nearly £19,000 worth. No one man could do it. Without some such organisation as had been devised, the thing would be out of the question.

And then French saw that he had made a mistake. This consideration did not answer his question. For every half-crown Welland gave the girls, he received one in exchange. How did he get rid of these latter? *How did he get rid of them?*

He simply could not do it! He had been watched too carefully. French did not believe he could have passed even small things like packages of "snow." How much less comparatively bulky bags of half-crowns! Once again French swore, this time half aloud.

"Beg pardon, Mr French?"

His attention was recalled to the girl, whom in his abstraction he had forgotten.

"Just a little habit of mine," he said, the twinkle reappearing in his eyes. "I think that's all I want. I'll take eighty of those half-crowns of Welland's and give you eighty of mine in exchange. Then you must carry on as usual."

"Very good, Mr French." She paused, then went on hesitatingly. "I wish you would tell me something about it. I don't suppose you could, of course, but I'm frightfully interested."

French glanced at her keenly, then smiled.

"I only wish I could," he answered pleasantly. "If I knew enough to answer your questions I'd be a much happier man. But I'll soon know all about it and I'll tell you then. In any case, the less you know, the better for your own health." Then an idea occurred to him and he went on: "Tell me, do you go about London much?"

"Me? No, Mr French. What do you mean?"

"I mean, I should imagine that a young lady in your position with a free forenoon should take some exercise in the form of walks. Do you not explore the streets?"

"Oh, I see. Well, yes, I do a little, but I'm not a great walker."

"Very well. Avoid the neighbourhood of Waterloo Station and also Harrow."

She looked interested.

"I'll explain," went on French. "Mr Welland lives at Harrow and he garages his car in Tate's Lane off York Road. York Road is close to Waterloo. Now it might be disastrous if he saw you near either place, as he might imagine you were spying on him. So keep away from both districts."

French was in a thoughtful mood as he returned to the Yard. Seldom had he been up against so clear-cut a problem. Welland was getting hundreds of half-crowns each day; he must be getting rid of them somehow or he must be storing them somewhere; how, or where? It seemed impossible that there could be a difficulty in finding the solution. French was therefore the more exasperated by his failure to do so.

In a kind of dream he took the eighty half-crowns to the Mint. To a high official he told his story, with the result that immediate investigations and tests were put in hand. He had a long wait, but before he left he got his information. All the half-crowns were genuine; no such coins had been recalled to the Mint; no disused cellar existed in which such coins might have been kept; no half-crowns had been stolen.

This, of course, was final proof of the falsity of the tale Welland had told Molly, which so far as it went was to the good. But it made the entire operations of the gang even more inexplicable. If they were not getting rid of counterfeit coins, what under heaven were they doing? French's brain reeled as he faced the problem.

He walked slowly back to the Yard, full of bewilderment and baffled rage. These people were changing one lot of perfectly good half-crowns for another. In spite of the magnitude of the numbers dealt with, they were getting in no half-crowns from outside nor were they disposing of any. At least, they certainly were not obtaining nor distributing anything like the number passed by the girls. What was it all for?

A sudden wild hooting of a motor horn and frenzied cries from passers-by recalled French to his surroundings. He sprang practically from beneath the bonnet of a heavily laden bus — only just in time. For quite a hundred yards he forgot about Welland and his half-crowns as he meditated upon the undesirability of

171

dreaming in the London streets. Then his thoughts swung back again to his problem.

Whether it was due to the start he had received or whether it arose in the normal processes of thought, he immediately found himself considering a new idea. Suppose all these apparently contradictory premises were true? Suppose Welland *was* neither obtaining half-crowns nor disposing of them? Suppose he *was* changing one perfectly good lot of them for another? What if the half-crowns he obtained from the girls on one day were handed back to them on the next? What if this elaborate machinery was simply a blind to cover some more sinister proceedings? Had Molly Moran lied and were the gang selling drugs after all?

Admittedly, French did not see how such a scheme would facilitate the distribution of cocaine or heroin, but this problem seemed to him the lesser of the two. At all events, there must be more in it than half-crowns.

But lengthy pondering over it produced no light. Every solution that occurred to him seemed more improbable than the last.

In despair he returned to the idea that the disposal of the half-crowns was the essential. Suppose a hoard of half-crowns had been stolen, some of which were known to be marked? Most unlikely admittedly, but at least this theory covered the facts.

In his efforts to carry the thing a step further he tried a trick which had frequently helped him out of a similar tight place. If when following a trail of footsteps he came to hard ground on which they were not visible, he made a cast and went on to the next soft area in the hope of picking them up again. Now he made a mental cast. Assuming Welland were getting rid of these coins changed by the girls, and leaving out the means by which it was being done, what must be their eventual destination?

Long cogitation told him that the man's only plan must be to pay them into a bank. In no other way that French could see could he realise their value.

This at least opened out an obvious line of research. With a sense of relief at renewed action he drafted a circular to the managers of the various banks in London. He was anxious to trace a man who, he believed, was paying in large numbers of half-crowns to banks. He would be grateful to the manager if he would make inquiries as to whether such payments were being made at his bank, and if so, let him have some particulars on the matter.

For the remainder of that day the inquiry hung fire, but next morning French was called to the telephone. The manager of the Knightsbridge Branch of the London and County Bank believed that he had some information which might be useful to the inspector and would be glad if he would call round.

Half an hour later French was seated in the manager's private room.

"I do not know," said Mr Elwood, "whether I have brought you on a wild-goose chase, but for nearly a year a man has been paying in some four to six hundred half-crowns each Wednesday afternoon. It is common enough to have a weekly payment of silver, but uncommon to have it restricted to coins of one denomination. When, therefore, I received your circular I thought that it might be the man you wanted."

"Sounds hopeful," French agreed cheerily. "Perhaps you will give me the details?"

The manager touched a bell. "Mr Whitley," he said, as a dark, keen looking young man entered, "you might answer any questions that Mr French here asks you about Mr Welland, of Acacia Avenue, Harrow."

"Welland?" exclaimed French in amazement. "Is he a well-built, prosperous looking man with the typical American business-man type of face?"

"No, sir," returned the clerk. "Mr Welland is slight, with a pale complexion and a small, fair moustache. He has peculiar eyes, light blue and with a queer sort of stare."

A wave of excitement swept over French. "Style!" he thought, in high delight. Things were beginning to move at last!

"I think I recognise the man you mean, Mr Whitley," he said pleasantly, "though I knew him under another name. Now what about this Mr Welland? When did you come across him first?"

"He came in one day about a year ago." The clerk hesitated. "If I might get my books I could give you the exact date."

The manager nodded and in a few minutes the young man returned with a voluminous ledger.

"He first called on the 17th of August last and said he wished to open an account. You may remember, sir," Mr Whitley turned to the manager, "that I brought him in to you. He said that he carried on business as a bookmaker and that he dealt particularly in betting on dog-races. He had worked out a scheme whereby his bets were limited to half-crowns and multiples of a half-crown, with the result that he found himself with large numbers of half-crowns on his hands. His lodgments would therefore be made in coins of this denomination. On that day he lodged £60 worth of half-crowns. It was a Wednesday, and every Wednesday since then he has come in with amounts varying from fifty to a hundred pounds all in half-crowns."

"I follow you," said French. "I take it then that his account has been steadily growing?"

"No," the young man returned, "for he draws cheques for comparatively large amounts at intervals. I do not think that his account has ever stood at more than £500. When it amounts to from £400 to £500 he draws all out except a few pounds."

"By cheque?"

"Yes, by cheque."

"In whose favour?"

"In his own."

"I suppose I need scarcely ask you, Mr Whitley, if you were satisfied that this business was perfectly in order? Did it not strike you as strange that a man should lodge nothing but half-crowns?"

"Well, you see," the young man returned, "he explained that, otherwise I probably would have thought it odd."

"Then it is not an uncommon thing for silver to be lodged in that way?"

"Oh, no, quite common. Small shopkeepers and persons of that class generally make a weekly lodgment in silver, but of course it is in coins of all denominations."

"Quite. Does Mr Welland call about the same time each Wednesday?"

"Yes, always about two o'clock."

"Very good," said French. "With your permission, sir," he turned to the manager, "I shall be here at two o'clock next Wednesday, that is tomorrow, to meet Mr Welland. I may say that I believe the information you have given me will prove highly important and I need scarcely impress on you both the absolute importance of saying nothing of my visit and of giving no warning to Mr Welland."

French's mind was in a whirl as he left the bank. Then it *was* half-crowns! But what was the object of it all? He swore impotently as he came up once more against the problem.

But one thing at least was altogether splendid! For some time past he believed he had had sufficient evidence against Style to convict him of murder, but his difficulty had been that Style had vanished. Now Style was found, or at least he would be on the next day. That was two of the known members of the gang. With luck the shadowing of Style would lead him to the third, Gwen Lestrange. This morning had marked a great forward step in the investigation.

But when he reached the Yard, French's delight increased tenfold. There were there awaiting him two other telephone messages and two letters, all from the

176

managers of banks and all containing similar news. In each case the manager advised him that in reply to his circular he believed the wanted man was dealing at his bank, and each suggested a call for further information.

During the afternoon French was a busy man. Engaging a taxi, he drove round the various branches and in each found that Style was making a lodgment of half-crowns, exactly as had been described by Whitley at Knightsbridge. Only on one point did the stories differ. Each bank was visited by Style on a different day of the week. Monday, Tuesday, Wednesday, Friday and Saturday's visits were accounted for, and on ringing up the Yard from the last branch he visited French was able to place Thursday's call also. A similar communication had come in from still another bank.

With this information he felt that he should soon reach a decisive stage in the case. Style once located, the end was in sight.

But he racked his brains in exasperation as his former problem recurred to him. Again, how was Welland passing these coins to Style? The more French thought over the investigation he had made, the more impossible it seemed that the man could be doing it. And yet here was definite proof that it was being done daily.

He sat down at his desk and, contrary to his usual custom in the office, lit his pipe and began to smoke with long, steady pulls, as he gave himself up to thought. For the nth time he visualised the whole proceedings; the placing of the coins in the secret panel of the car by the girls; the driving of the car to the garage; Welland's walk to his office; his journey to Harrow; his game of golf; his return next day to his office; his walk to the garage and the taking out of the car. Every one of these had been checked and rechecked so often that it was impossible — *impossible* — that the coins could have been got rid of. And yet they had been.

French wondered if he could not narrow the issue. The coins definitely reached the garage, because observation showed that they were not taken out of the car in the streets. Though it was by no means demonstrated, he inclined to the opinion that when Welland left the garage he did not take the coins with him. The man seldom carried anything in his hand, and so bulky a package could scarcely have been placed in his pocket without causing a bulge. But no bulge had been observed. It certainly looked, therefore, as if the coins were being left in the garage.

Though his examination had been exhaustive, French again racked his brains as to whether he could not have overlooked some means of access to the garage. Then suddenly an idea occurred to him which filled him once again with the eager enthusiasm which every forward step in an investigation produced.

The drain! Could the drain be a fake? Could it represent the communication he wanted? He determined that that very night he would examine it again.

Accordingly two o'clock next morning saw him repeat with Sergeant Ormsby the proceedings of three weeks earlier. Waiting until the policeman had turned out of Tate's Lane, they swarmed over the coachbuilder's wall, and creeping to the garage, let themselves in with Ormsby's key.

"I'm not satisfied about this drain, Ormsby," French explained. "I want to make sure that there is nothing more here than meets the eye. Let's have this cover up again."

They raised the manhole cover and Ormsby got into the inspection chamber and prepared to examine the three pipes in turn. French, lying down in the pit, was able to put his eye to that connecting the pit to the chamber. Ormsby's torch lit it completely, so that every inch was visible. It was a perfectly clear connection without any break or junction and French had to admit that nothing was to be learned from it.

The second pipe from the chamber was the outfall with the intercepting trap attached. Here also investigation showed that everything was as it should be. The trap was full of water, and on Ormsby removing the disc sealing the pipe immediately above it, a rush of offensive gases came out, proving that the connection to the sewer was genuine.

There remained therefore only the ventilating pipe and this, it was obvious, passed under the floor to the vertical shaft and so to the roof.

"That is all right, Mr French. You needn't worry about it. It is just an ordinary vent pipe," Ormsby declared.

But French still was not satisfied.

"I must make sure of the connection," he said. "Couldn't you get up on the roof, Ormsby, and pour down some water and see if it comes out here?"

The pipe passed out through the roof at the back of the garage, opposite the door. With some difficulty Ormsby climbed on the wall between the yard and the adjoining property, then shuffling up the roof, poured down the pipe the canful of water which French handed up. A gurgling sound followed by a rush of water into the inspection chamber showed immediately that the connection was good.

"Curse it all," thought French in disgust, "this darned thing is no good either. I suppose it must be that confounded office after all."

"Did it come all right?" said Ormsby, re-entering the garage and looking into the inspection chamber. "I thought you wouldn't get anything there, Mr French. The thing is perfectly normal." He climbed down once more into the inspection chamber and began pushing his rule up the ventilating pipe.

French watched him idly while he stood racking his brains over the problem. Then a sudden exclamation from Ormsby attracted his attention.

"What's the matter?" he asked sharply. "Got anything?"

"I'm not so sure, Mr French. Here's a queer thing and no mistake."

"What is it?" said French, bending over the chamber.

"Why here." Ormsby measured the distance along the floor from the chamber to the vertical pipe. It was just three feet four.

"Now see here," he said.

Again he got into the chamber and pushed the rule into the horizontal pipe. French watched breathlessly as the three-foot rule disappeared and after it was the man's entire arm!

"There you are, Mr French," Ormsby declared. "That pipe goes through. The vent pipe is only fixed on to a tee, not a bend. Let's find how far it goes."

Eagerly Ormsby went out, and looking round the yard, brought in some thin laths. One of these he pushed up the pipe, then tying on the others, like lengths of a fishing rod, pushed the whole in. It made a length of about ten feet — three times the distance to the vertical pipe. At the end of the ten feet it brought up against something hard.

"What's the idea, Ormsby? What can that pipe be for?"

"Not for ventilation, Mr French, I'll swear. If it only went a foot beyond the vertical pipe I shouldn't be so sure, for the builder might have had an old tee that he wanted to use. But this has been carried on deliberately for at least another five feet."

"Through the wall!"

"Through the wall. I'd like to see the end of that pipe in the next lot."

French swore delightedly.

"So you shall, Ormsby," he chuckled. "We'll get across now and have a look. Get your sticks out and this manhole cover on so that the place'll be as we found it."

They removed the traces of their visit, and shutting off their torches, crept out once more into the darkness of the night.

CHAPTER
FOURTEEN

The Property Adjoining

The two men halted when they had relocked the door behind them, looking around and listening.

The night was intensely dark. A thick pall of cloud cut off all light from the sky, even the meagre light of the stars. Above the wall bounding Tate's Lane they could see the upper stories of the houses opposite, lit up faintly by the street lamps. Elsewhere not a gleam of light showed. It was silent also. Save for the complaining call of a marauding cat and the distant whistle of a train, no sound broke the stillness.

Satisfied that they were unobserved, Ormsby made a "back" and French swung himself up on the wall dividing the two properties. Ormsby followed and both men dropped softly to the ground at the other side.

"This is what we want," whispered French as he felt along a building beside them. "Here's where our pipe goes to all right."

It was another shed, identical, so far as they could make out in the darkness, with the garage and set end to end with it.

"We must get in," went on French. "Have a try at the lock."

"It's a chubb like the other," returned Ormsby. "There's not much chance of getting it open." He fumbled for a moment, then: "By Jove! I can do it after all. The same key fits both. Here you are, Mr French. A bit of luck, that is."

"It's proof the same parties are running the two, though we scarcely needed that. Come in and close the door."

The door shut, French cautiously turned on his torch. The shed was a garage, identical in design with Welland's. Here were the same cement-finished walls and floor, the same window, pit and bench, the same manhole cover and ventilating pipe. There was no car, but there was something a good deal more interesting. Hanging from hooks beneath the bench was a twelve-foot sewer cleaners' "serpent," a flexible rod with a pair of toothed jaws at one end operated by a bowden wire from the other.

"There," said French, pointing to the rod, "there's the proof we wanted. That's what he uses to get the bags of half-crowns through the pipe. But to set the thing beyond doubt, Ormsby, you better go back into the other garage and flash your light into the pipe. I'll watch this end."

While he was away, French made a sketch of the pipes for his report. A copy is given here.

Presently a muffled voice came from the drain and French, crouching down in the inspection chamber, saw Ormsby's torch in the distance.

"That's that," French whispered down the pipe. "Come back and we'll have a look round here."

They now essayed a more difficult task. Starting from the garage, they felt their way along the various walls, pacing their lengths and estimating the angles between them. It was not easy work in the dark, but French was too much afraid of being overlooked to use his torch. When they had worked round to their starting point they returned to the garage, where French made a sketch from his measurements.

The area appeared to be a yard, irregular in shape and surrounded by buildings. From the nature of the debris which filled one corner, old crates mostly, the place seemed more like a shop or works than a private house. Opposite the garage an arched roadway passed under one of the buildings, ending in a pair of close-sheeted gates. A gleam of light beneath the gates indicated that they opened on to a street.

"I want to mark that entrance gate," French said as he put away his sketch. "We must locate it in the street outside." He paused in thought. "I have it," he went on. "Here is a penny. We'll push it out underneath and then go round and see if we can find it."

They carried out this programme. Having made sure that they had left no traces of their visit, they locked the garage, pushed the penny beneath the large gate, and climbed back, first into the builder's yard and then into Tate's Lane. Then walking round the block to the parallel street, Killowen Street, they began searching for a likely gateway. There were a number of such, but at the third they found their penny and knew that they had reached their goal.

The entrance stood beside a shop, and when French read its signboard he felt amazed and puzzled. It bore the legend, "Theobald & Grudgin. Working Silversmiths."

"Je-hosaphat! Can it be coining after all?" he whispered in bewilderment. If so, what about the report from the Mint? That report amounted to practical proof that counterfeit coins were not being passed. And now here was, at least, extremely suggestive evidence that they were! He swore his comprehensive oath, but it scarcely brought its customary relief.

"Looks to me as if those Mint people had been diddled — like ourselves," he muttered. "Well, Ormsby, that's all we can do now. We'll get off home."

He wondered if it would be wise after all to return to the silversmiths' next morning, or rather that morning, for it was after four o'clock. What he wanted was to get his hands on Style; the activities at the silversmiths' could wait. If he went to Theobald & Grudgin's he might be seen by some member of the gang. The alarm would then be given and the gang might disperse, greatly increasing the difficulties of rounding them up. No, on second thoughts he would lie low for the morning. He would visit the bank at two o'clock and there either arrest Style or shadow him to his home, the latter probably, as it might lead him to Gwen Lestrange and perhaps still other members of the gang.

But next morning a fresh development took place which banished all thoughts of finesse and sent him hotfoot to the silversmiths' and any other place from which news of the trio might be obtained.

He had been busy at routine work in connection with the case. He had begun by ringing up the inspector of the York Road district to ask for such information as might be available about Messrs Theobald & Grudgin and their establishment. Then he had gone down to the Mint to report his discovery and to ask as tactfully as he could whether a mistake might not have been made in their half-crown diagnosis.

The very senior officer who received him had been emphatic in his reply. No mistake could possibly have been made. The tests gave absolutely conclusive results. Silversmiths or no silversmiths, the coins he had sent them were genuine.

Scarcely had French retured to the Yard when the blow fell. As he sat down at his desk his telephone rang.

"Is that Mr French, the inspector?" asked a woman's voice which French vaguely remembered, but could not place. "I'm Mrs Creuse, of 27 Nelson Street."

Nelson Street! Of course, the proprietor of Molly Moran's boarding house.

"Yes, Mrs Creuse. Inspector French speaking. Anything I can do for you?"

"It's about Miss Moran," the voice went on. "She did not come back after the performance last night and I'm anxious about her. I shouldn't have thought anything about it only for your inquiries here. A girl sometimes goes home with friends and is not always careful to ring up her boarding house. But she was always careful that way."

French's heart almost stood still for a moment. Was it possible . . .? Could these infernal scoundrels have got hold of her as they got hold of Thurza Darke and her two unhappy predecessors?

"Did you not ring up the cinema?" he asked quickly.

"Yes, but by the time I began to get anxious it was too late. You see, it's often nearly twelve before Miss Moran gets home, and it was only by chance that I was up myself about one and discovered she had not arrived. I rang up the cinema first thing this morning, but I've only just got through. They say she never turned up to business yesterday. I hope she's all right."

French stiffened, sure that this confirmed his worst fears. Why, *why* had not the Panopticon people rung him up? Grimly he promised himself a straight talk with the manager. But that could wait. Now the urgent matter was to organise a search. In times of emergency French always rose to the occasion. Pausing only to ring up the Panopticon for confirmation of the landlady's statement, he set to work. For some thirty seconds he sat motionless, staring with unseeing eyes at the polished wood of his desk, while he rapidly considered the measures he would take. Then deliberately, but without the loss of a moment, he proceeded to put his plans into operation.

His first step was to hurry to Chief Inspector Mitchell's room, tell him the news and outline his proposals for dealing with the situation. French already held warrants for the arrest of all three known members of the gang, but he now wanted search warrants for Welland's house and office as well as for the premises of the silversmiths, Messrs Theobald & Grudgin. With all his proposals Mitchell expressed his agreement.

187

French next summoned a number of men to his room.

"I think you all know something of the case I'm on," he began, speaking in quiet but impressive tones. "Starting with the Portsmouth murder, I have found that a gang of crooks have murdered three cinema pay-box girls whom they feared were about to give away their secrets to the police. Now I've just had a 'phone that a fourth girl has disappeared — a Miss Molly Moran, employed in the pay office of the Panopticon Cinema in Leicester Square. You have seen her, Carter, and also you, Harvey. She got into the clutches of the gang, same as the other three girls, and has been working for them. Only the day before yesterday she told me her story, and it looks as if they may have got wise to it and done her in."

He paused and the men nodded in silence.

"She left her boarding house in Nelson Street, so I am advised, at her usual time yesterday morning and has not been heard of since. If these people have got her you will see that we can't lose any time."

Again the men nodded and French went on with his directions.

"You, Carter, will take two men and bring in Curtice Welland. Here is a warrant which I have had ready for some time. Here is his description and the places, so far as we know, where he is likely to be found. I leave all the details to you. But no bungling! Bring him in, and quickly."

Sergeant Carter promptly disappeared and French turned to the next in the line.

"I want you, Harvey, to go into the affair at the Panopticon Cinema. You may get a line on some caller or hear of a letter or telephone. Advise the Yard if you have any luck."

Harvey disappeared in his turn and French resumed.

"You, Pickford, try the boarding house. Here is the address and all particulars. I need scarcely prompt you. You know what to do."

So the wheels of the ponderous machine of the C.I.D. began to creak and relentlessly the great trap was set. In addition to Carter and his helpers, men were sent to watch all the places which Welland was known to frequent: his house, his office, the garage, his golf club. Inquiries were to be made from his housekeeper, the other occupiers of the office buildings, the staff in the coachbuilder's yard and the secretary and other members of the golf club. The three other girls known to be in the clutches of the gang were to be shadowed, and any member of the gang seen approaching them was instantly to be secured. Men were to be despatched to each of the six banks at which Style had lodged half-crowns, in case he should be seized with a desire to withdraw his money. The last inquiry French reserved for himself. "Ormsby," he concluded, "you and I will go and have a look round that silversmiths' yard. I've got a search warrant, but I'll not use it if I can avoid it. Better get a couple of men to watch the door while we're inside."

Fifteen minutes later French and Ormsby turned into Killowen Street and walked in a leisurely way towards Messrs Theobald & Grudgin's establishment.

The big gate under which they had pushed the penny was open and without hesitation they entered. The entry led through the house to the yard at the back. In the corner immediately opposite stood the garage, and from it, across the back end of the yard, ran the wall separating the premises from the coachbuilder's establishment adjoining. The remaining sides were bounded by buildings, all dirty and in bad repair. Three doors, one open, gave on the yard. Another door, apparently from the office or shop, opened into the side wall of the entry. The yard also was dirty and heaps of old boxes and other rubbish lay in corners.

French stood for a moment motionless, taking in these details and noting with satisfaction the accuracy of his sketch plan. Then he walked slowly to the open door.

He found himself on the threshold of a fair-sized workshop, fitted up with several benches and a few simple looking machines. In one corner stood a gas oven with crucibles, presumably for melting the silver. Close by was what looked like a tiny foundry. Several of the benches bore small lathes but most of the simple machinery was for smoothing and polishing. The place looked as if at one time it might have been busy and successful, but now it had been allowed to go to seed. Like the yard, it was dirty and untidy and its entire staff consisted of three old men, dirty and untidy also, and clearly past their work. One was busy at the gas oven as if about to make a cast, the others were filing up and polishing silver ornaments.

"Could I see the manager?" French asked after giving the men a pleasant good morning.

The man from the gas oven turned off a tap and slowly approached.

"'E ain't in yet, so far as I knows," he said. "You've tried the office?"

"Not there," French declared mendaciously.

"Aye. Well, 'e ain't come in. 'E usually comes in in 'is car abaht ten or 'alf past, but this morning 'e ain't turned up yet. Was you wanting anything."

"Yes. I want a quotation for a silver trowel and casket for laying a foundation stone. But I expect I'd better see the boss about it."

"Aye," said the man again. "There ain't no one 'ere as could tell you abaht that. Take a seat in the office, mister. The boss won't be long."

"I can wait. I'm not in a hurry." French took out his cigarette case and held it out. "I think I know your boss," he resumed conversationally, "but I'm hanged if I haven't forgotten his name. He's a rather slight man of middle height with a pale complexion and a small fair moustache, isn't he? Rather staring eyes?"

"That's 'im, mister. You've 'it 'im off 'bout proper. Welland, they calls 'im. Mr Curtice Welland."

"Welland! Of course. I remember now. Lives out at Harrow?"

"Blowed if I could tell. 'E ain't never asked me 'ome to dinner."

"That's his loss," said French with a smile. He glanced casually round the workshop. "Fine place you have here. Too big for three men surely?"

The old man shook his head despondingly.

"It were a good shop once, but times is not wot they were. I've seen the day when there were twenty men working in this 'ere shop and doing good work and plenty of it. And now there's only three of us left and there ain't much for us to do neither. It were a bad day for us when the old master sold out."

"Then the works have changed hands?"

"Aye, abaht a year ago. Old Mr Grudgin 'ad it; Mr Theobald, 'e's dead this five year. I s'pose Mr Grudgin were feeling it too much for 'im; 'e were seventy if 'e were a day. So 'e sold it to this 'ere Mr Welland and," the old man paused, finally adding, "some'ow the work fell off and most of the men were sacked. But Lord knows I ain't got no cause to complain! I'm 'ere still, though younger men than me got the boot."

"It's been a terrible time for trade right enough," French declared sympathetically. "And yours is what you might call a luxury trade, so you would feel bad times worse then most."

"That's right, mister."

"What kind of work do you do mostly?" went on French with the forced interest of a man who has time to put away.

"We used to do all kinds, statuettes and plaques and trophy cups and vases and medallions and such like. But we don't so much now; lids for inkpots and penholders and backs for fancy clothes brushes and stoppers for toilet bottles for suitcases: that's abaht all."

"I suppose Mr Welland looks after sales himself? You haven't a traveller?"

192

"No, there ain't nobody now but Mr Welland and the boy wot you saw in the office."

French chatted on in a leisurely way, moving about the shop as he did so. He did not learn much from the man's conversation, but he satisfied himself that, except possibly in some secret cellar, no coining was in progress. Such articles as still were being made, so the old man assured him, went from the workshop to the office, where Welland, to give him that name, disposed of them. Of this side of the business the workmen knew nothing. The silver came in the form of bars or ingots, usually by motor lorry. It was stored in the shed adjoining Welland's garage, a strongly built shed of which only Welland had the key. Where it came from the man did not know.

Seeing that no further information was to be had, French explained that he did not think he could wait for Mr Welland that day, but that he would call again. Then wishing the old man good day, he left the yard.

Ormsby was waiting for him in the archway.

"Style's running this place under the name of Welland," French said to him in a low tone. "Took it over about a year ago. It seems there's a boy in the office. I'm going to make a search. Come in with me."

Ormsby nodded and the two men, passing out into the street, turned into the shop.

A glass door which rang a bell on being opened, led into a dark and untidy showroom. Across the front was a counter, with behind it a row of show cases containing plaster models. These cases acted as a screen, cutting off the office portion behind. In the background were a small green safe, a letter file and two desks. One, a roll top, was closed, the other was a high desk with a brass rail bookstand above. The back wall was pierced by a window giving on to the yard, while in the side wall was the door leading to the entry. Some dirty calendars and advertisement plates hung crookedly here and there.

At the high desk sat a youth of about twenty with a pen in his hand and a ledger spread out before him. French thought he had never seen anyone in the position of clerk who looked so utterly devoid of intelligence. He watched him make a clumsy attempt to hide a well-thumbed novelette with a lurid picture on the cover, then said pleasantly: "Could I see Mr Welland, please?"

The youth pushed the novelette into his pocket and slowly advanced to the counter.

"'E ain't 'ere," he replied succinctly.

"So I observe," said French, looking carefully round the room. "Do you know when he will be in?"

"Naw."

French fixed the youth with a severe eye.

"Now, sonny," he said sharply. "We're police officers and we're looking for Mr Welland. When was he here last?"

The youth gaped and it took a repetition of the question in a still sharper tone to wake him up.

"Yesterday morning," he answered sullenly.

Style, it appeared, had arrived at the works at his usual hour, about half past ten. Customarily he remained till one o'clock, when he left for lunch. But on this occasion he had only waited a few minutes. He had sent the youth out on a message, and when the latter had returned half an hour later he had disappeared. The youth had not seen him since.

French was not satisfied.

"What was the message?" he asked.

It was a bow drawn at a venture with the general object of amassing detailed knowledge, but to his amazement the arrow got in between the joints of Style's armour.

"Postal order for two bob," the youth returned.

"That shouldn't have taken you half an hour."

"'E didn't want no order," the youth declared, and his eyes looked sly and furtive. "'E only wanted me out of the way."

"What makes you think that?"

The youth smiled, a sort of sickly leer, unpleasant to look upon.

"The gal," he remarked laconically.

"The girl? What girl?"

"The gal as came in with him."

"A tall, strong, well-built girl with fair hair and complexion and blue eyes?" French suggested eagerly, believing he was on the track of Gwen Lestrange.

"Naw. Small and dark."

French leaped to his feet.

"What?" he roared, scaring the youth almost into fits.

Molly Moran! He paused, thrilled at the thought, then sat down again.

"That's all right," he declared. "I was surprised for the moment. Now tell me all about this girl. When did she come?"

Getting information from the youth was like getting treacle out of a test-tube, but by the exercise of all his patience French managed it.

It seemed that when Style had arrived he had driven his car into the yard with his usual custom. It was a dark green Armstrong-Siddeley saloon. But instead of garaging it he had turned it and run it back into the entry, stopping opposite the office door. Then he had hurried back to the street. Evidently Molly — further questions had left French in no doubt as to the "gal's" identity — had been waiting for him, for both came at once into the office. Style had asked her to sit down and had then excused himself on urgent business in the workshops. In a few moments the speaking tube from the workshops had whistled. It was Style and he had instructed the youth to go out immediately and buy a two-shilling postal order. Such a thing had never been asked for before and the youth did not believe it was required. He had therefore assumed that the errand was to get him out of the way in order to allow the tender passages between Style and his caller which he imagined were desired. In this belief he had improved the opportunity to visit a friend, the message boy in a neighbouring shop, and he was not back for half an hour. Style and the young lady had then gone.

French made a despairing gesture.

"After my warning! After my warning!" he lamented in a low voice to Ormsby. "How under the sun did that scoundrel get her into his power?"

He turned again to the youth.

196

"We're going to search this place," he said sharply. "Here's our warrant, if you'd like to see it. Now hand over any keys you have, then sit down there and don't interfere."

As he spoke he shut and bolted the heavy outer door. Then ruthlessly silencing the clerk's timid protests, the two men began the search.

The safe was beyond them and French put through a call to the Yard for an expert. The roll top desk, however, was easily overcome by means of French's skeleton keys. Quickly, but thoroughly, the two men turned the place out. For a couple of hours they worked, first in the office and then in the workshops behind, before French announced that he was satisfied.

Though the search had yielded little, that little was important. No hint as to Style's possible whereabouts had been gained nor any information as to the remaining members of the gang. Still less was there any hint as to what might have happened to Molly Moran, though French's sketch of the tracks of Style's car and its detailed description, obtained from the old workman, might later on help in tracing her. But two things had been made clear beyond possibility of doubt. First, the silversmiths' business was practically non-existent. It was evidently a mere blind to cover more serious and lucrative operations. Secondly, though scarcely any silver articles had been sold, the purchase of bar silver had been very large.

Report from the Mint or no report, there could no longer be any doubt as to what was being done. Coining on an enormous scale was in progress. The next thing for French must be to find the plant. Or rather the next thing but one. At all costs Molly Moran's life must be saved, were this humanly possible.

While French was sitting in his office turning these matters over in his mind, the Yard expert had not been idle. He now called to them that he had just succeeded in opening the safe. French began eagerly to go through its contents. But he found only one thing of interest, four little leathern bags shaped to fit the divisions in the vanity bags, each containing from a hundred to a hundred and fifty half-crowns.

Sure that at last he held the key to the affair, he poured the coins out on to the desk and examined them minutely. Immediately he was once again disappointed. All of them, he was prepared to swear, were genuine. Every test he applied proved them so. And then suddenly he wondered. All of them were dated 1921!

Whether this meant anything or not he did not know, but it was at least certain that they must at once be sent to the Mint for an authoritative opinion.

More anxious then ever as to Molly's fate, French returned to the Yard, hoping against hope that some useful information might have come in.

CHAPTER
FIFTEEN

Mr Cullimore Expounds

French was profoundly worried by the disappearance of Molly Moran. He could not get out of his mind the thought that if anything happened to her he was by no means free from responsibility. There could be no doubt that it was through him that she had incurred the suspicion of the gang, and he had led her to believe that she could confide in him with perfect safety. Bitterly he regretted his oversight in not having her shadowed so that her kidnapping would have been impossible. Again and again he cursed his mistake and again and again he swore to leave no stone unturned to save her, and if unhappily he failed in that, to bring her murderers to justice.

There was little that he could do personally but remain in his room and collate and sift the information which soon began to come in. A good deal was obtained as a result of the inquiries which he had set on foot, but unfortunately it was all negative.

The first news he had was from the men he had sent to the banks at which Style got rid of his half-crowns. At none of them had the man been seen. This was Thursday and since Tuesday he had neither paid in half-crowns nor drawn cheques. The total sum standing to his credit in all six was close on five hundred pounds. It was evident, therefore, that he was badly frightened, if, as seemed likely, he had abandoned the money.

Telephone reports from the other men engaged were equally disappointing. Sergeant Harvey rang up to say that he had been unable to learn anything at the Panopticon. Miss Moran had left at her usual time on the Tuesday evening and an assistant with whom she had walked to the tube said that her remarks showed that she intended to be at work on the following day. Nor was any news available from her boarding house. On the Wednesday evening she had not returned after the performance. That was the desolating fact. She had not sent any message to explain her absence nor had she previously given a hint to anyone there that she might not be home.

Even more disquieting was the report from Carter. He had been unable to arrest Curtice Welland because Welland also had disappeared. The man had not returned home on Wednesday evening nor had he been seen since. His housekeeper, however, was not alarmed about him as he had sent her a telegram on Wednesday afternoon to say that he was unexpectedly called away on business and would be absent for a few days. His usual haunts had been shadowed and exhaustive inquiries made, but all to no purpose.

The three other box office girls who had been changing coins were interrogated, also without result. At first all three had denied that they had been engaged in questionable practices with half-crowns, but the police examination had soon broken them down and they had admitted their complicity. But all stated that Wednesday was the last day on which they had seen Welland. None of them had seen Style for many weeks.

One vitally important piece of information, however, came in, a piece, indeed, fundamental to the whole inquiry. At any other time it would have raised French to the pitch of exalted enthusiasm usual to him under such circumstances. But now he was so worried about Molly Moran's safety that he took the news as a matter of course.

Returning to the Yard from a further visit to the girl's boarding house in Nelson Street, he found himself in demand. "Chief wants you, sir," he was told by the first three men he met, while Inspector Tanner, whom he passed on the way to his room, hailed him with, "Hullo, French, my son! Now you've been and gone and done it! There has been no peace here this morning, looking for Brer French."

Before French could reply a sergeant approached.

"Beg pardon, sir, but the assistant commissioner wishes to see you in his room as soon as possible."

"Lord!" said French. "What's all the shindy about? Right, Sergeant. I'm going now."

Sir Mortimer Ellison, the assistant commissioner, was seated at his desk in his well but plainly furnished office when French entered. With him were two other men, evidently from their dress and bearing persons of importance. One was small, white-haired and precise looking, the other, a younger man, was evidently his subordinate. All three were smoking the opulent

Turkish cigarettes which Sir Mortimer affected. The elder of the visitors was speaking, the others listening with every appearance of interest.

"Come along, French," said Sir Mortimer, interrupting the other's flow of conversation. "You've turned up in the nick of time. This is the inspector who has been handling the case, gentlemen. French, these are Mr Cullimore and Mr Dove from the Mint. They've called about that silver bombshell you sent down."

"What, sir?" French exclaimed. "Then the coins were counterfeit all right?"

"All right?" Sir Mortimer waved his hand towards French and looked quizzically at the others. "Hear Scotland Yard speak! French, you've got a distorted mind. Revelling in iniquity. Why should you be pleased because the revered institution which our friends represent has been the victim of a fraud?"

French knew his superior.

"Pleased to tell them, sir, that thanks to Scotland Yard the fraud is at an end," he said without a smile.

"There's Scotland Yard again. When you have no answer, beg the question. I do it myself, so I know. Now, French, sit down in that chair and tell us all about it."

But French remained standing with a puzzled expression on his face.

"But what about —" he began, then stopped.

"What is it, French?"

"Sorry, sir. But this can only refer to the second lot of coins. The first lot were good."

"That is so," broke in Cullimore in thin, precise tones. "The first batch was good. It is this second batch alone that is in question."

"A bit puzzling that, sir," French went on to the assistant commissioner. "I should have expected it the other way round. The first batch was given to the girl Moran to pass out to the public, the second was in Style's safe. Why should they pass out good coins?"

"You've got them the wrong way round. That lot you got from the girl must have been received from the public, not from the gang."

French shook his head.

"No, sir, I'm quite sure of my ground there. Miss Moran put the coins she got from the public in the car. What she gave me were taken from the car for distribution."

There was silence for a moment, then Sir Mortimer spoke.

"Well, if I can't prove you in the wrong I must try something else. How would this do? Those people are smarter than you've been giving them credit for. They twigged you were on them and went canny. Is there any way they could have known what you were up to?"

"Through the girls, sir," French admitted. "I saw the risk, but I had to take it."

"There you are, then. The girls reported your activities and Welland, Style & Co., thought it healthier to trade good money. Well, French, when these gentlemen rang me up to make an appointment I expected Chief Inspector Mitchell would be here to post me in the affair until you got back. But Mitchell has been detained at Croydon so that I have been unable to tell them more than the main outlines. Now you start in from the beginning and let us have all the details."

"About the cinema girls, sir?"

"About the silver. I've explained the method of distribution through the cinema girls and that is all these gentlemen require to know on that point. You tell about everything connected directly with the silver."

"I'm afraid, sir, there's not so much to be told. All I've found is —" and French began explaining his investigations in detail. He told of the distribution and transport of the coins, the vanity bags, the secret panel beneath the seat of Welland's car and the pipe connecting the two garages. Then he read out his notes of what he had found in the office, particularly the weights of silver and copper purchased compared to the weight of silver ornaments sold. The three men listened with keen attention, Cullimore congratulating him warmly when he had finished.

"It's the cleverest fraud I've come across for many a day," he declared. "Indeed I don't mind admitting that if it hadn't been for our friend here it might have gone on almost indefinitely. It would never have been discovered from mere inspection of the coins. They look perfect. Only careful tests in our laboratories proved they were counterfeit."

"Made by an expert?" Sir Mortimer prompted.

"Unquestionably. Perfectly marvellous the way they were turned out! I have shown them to several of our people and they all said they were good; men with wide experience too. I don't wonder that Miss Moran's bank clerk friend was deceived. You see," Cullimore monopolised the conversation with evident pleasure, "there are four principal tests of a silver coin: its appearance, by which I include feel and texture as well as design; its weight, its composition and its ring. All these tests were met or discounted, except perhaps that of composition and that was practically met."

"I don't know that I quite follow you," said Sir Mortimer, and French nodded his agreement.

"Well, take composition. The composition of these coins was the actual composition of the coins we turn out from the Mint. In other words, the fake coins were genuine as far as the material of which they were made was concerned — at least, as nearly as it could be done without our extraordinarily accurate system of proportioning the ingredients. In fact, it took our extraordinarily accurate system to discover the inaccuracy. That is what I meant by saying that this test of composition had been practically met."

The assistant commissioner nodded.

"The proportions of metal in our silver at present," went on Cullimore, "are 50 per cent silver and 50 per cent alloy, principally copper. You will see what I mean when I tell you that these fake coins contained not less than 48.63 nor more than 51.12 per cent of silver, the remainder being alloy. Nothing there to call one's attention to a fake!"

"That is so. Yet your people found the discrepancy."

Cullimore shrugged his shoulders.

"We did, but we're not proud of it. The less we say about that part of the affair the better. My point is that no one would have suspected anything wrong from the appearance of the coins."

Sir Mortimer nodded again.

"You mentioned three other tests?"

"Yes, those of design, weight and ring. Take the first of these. Now I'm sure you know, Sir Mortimer, that no matter how carefully a coin is copied, defects will creep in. Particles of dust or slight defects in the original will make a difference. Admittedly these may be invisible to the naked eye, but a microscope will reveal them. Any coins struck as copies, that is, not from the original dies, will be microscopically defective in the detail of its design. You follow me?"

"Quite."

"Now take weight. This is dependent primarily on the thickness of the coin and the correct thickness can only be produced by the elaborate machines in the Mint. It is scarcely conceivable that a forger could obtain one of these machines. These two tests together are therefore very reliable and convincing."

"Then surely the fake coins could have been discovered by these?"

"Ah," Cullimore replied, making a little gesture of demonstration as he reached his point, "that's what I thought you'd say and that's where the cleverness of this gang comes in. They discounted these two tests, and that in the simplest and most natural way imaginable. They wore the coins."

"Wore them?"

"Yes. In some way which we can only imagine they produced wear. Our engineers imagine that they turned them with very fine sand in some kind of a rotary churn, for the microscope shows that the wear is really caused by numbers of very fine scores and cuts. Ordinary wear from circulation, while it shows occasional cuts and scratches, leaves a comparatively smooth surface on the higher parts of the design. But even so, what I might call this counterfeiting of wear was uncommonly well done. Here again only the microscope could have told the difference."

"And that had the effect —"

"Yes," interrupted Cullimore, determined not to be cheated of his climax. "Don't you see? That had the effect of blurring the design so that minor defects became invisible and also lightening it so that the weight test became inoperative. Clever, wasn't it?"

"Rather an obvious precaution, I should say," the assistant commissioner commented, annoyed at having the words taken out of his mouth.

"No doubt," the other admitted, "but how to do it is not so obvious."

"Well, it's all very interesting at all events. What about the ring?"

Cullimore sat back and became less enthusiastic.

"The ring?" he repeated. "The ring is not so easy to explain. It depends on a lot of things, such as the precise degree of hardness of the coins. Even with the careful manufacture in the Mint we do not get all coins to ring alike. All have to be tested individually, and those which do not ring correctly are rejected. I fancy our counterfeiters must have adopted the same plan."

When Cullimore finished speaking there was silence for some seconds. Sir Mortimer busied himself in handing round fresh cigarettes. When they were lighted, French said:

"There is one point which has been bothering me since I became satisfied that these people were coining and that is, How does it pay them? Surely it must cost at least nearly half a crown to produce a half-crown?"

"No," returned Cullimore, "it doesn't. That's just the point. It should pay them uncommonly well. You know, of course," he went on, addressing the company generally, "that during the War the price of silver went up, so that coins were worth more when melted down than as currency. This actually led to a considerable loss of coins. To meet the difficulty the percentage of silver was reduced. Formerly it was 92.5 per cent, but in 1920 it was reduced to the 50 per cent of which I spoke a moment ago. Since 1920 the price of silver has fallen again. It is now standing at about two shillings an ounce. The cost of the silver in a half-crown is therefore less than sixpence — let us assume sixpence. The alloy and manufacture, including overhead, might at the very most be another sixpence. These people could therefore produce a half-crown at a cost of about a shilling, making eighteenpence profit on each coin. As the law now stands, that's the unhappy fact."

"By Jove!" French turned to Sir Mortimer. "In that case, sir, it prompts one to ask why the staple industry of the British Isles is not counterfeiting coining?"

"A pertinent question, French. I was considering it myself. Difficulty of distribution, I presume."

"That's it, Sir Mortimer," Cullimore declared. "Any skilful man may produce sufficiently good coins to pass, but it takes a genius to get rid of enough to pay for the plant. That's why most people with these ideas try printing notes. If you can make eight or nine shillings for every ten-shilling note you pass the game becomes worthwhile, particularly when changing notes is so easy. But you cannot change half-crowns in the same way. Some system of changing like that of Mr French's friends becomes necessary and that's where the trouble arises."

"That's where it arose in this case anyway," said French. "The distribution was the weak link in the whole scheme."

"So it has proved," Cullimore admitted. "But I consider it an extremely clever scheme all the same. The more you consider the problem involved, the more you will realise, I think, its enormous difficulty. Just think, Mr French. How would you have done it?"

"Oh, come now, Mr Cullimore," Sir Mortimer said gravely. "Don't make him incriminate himself. If you ask him questions like that you will have him telling you that things of the kind are not done at the Yard."

French grinned.

"That, sir, *is* the answer to the question. All the same if I had to find a scheme, I should try to avoid one which left me in the hands of four box office girls. That's what gave the thing away. If the girls had been members of the conspiracy it might never have come out. But the fear that the girls would give the show away led to them doing so."

"I begin to appreciate the force of your remark, Sir Mortimer, about the Yard's habit of begging the question," Cullimore declared dryly. "But I don't quite appreciate Mr French's point. You say, Mr French, that the girls gave the scheme away. But I understood they hadn't?"

"Not directly, sir. But the gang were afraid they might and adopted murder to safeguard themselves. The murder gave them away."

"Oh, quite. I see what you mean." Cullimore dismissed the point airily and turned to a new one. "I suppose there is no way of estimating how many of these faked half-crowns are in existence?"

"You gave me some figures on that, French. Just turn them up, will you?"

"All I can suggest is this, sir. Miss Moran told me that she passed out from one hunderd to one hundred and fifty a day. I took a minimum of between seven and eight hundred a week. If all four girls were doing the same that would be, say, three thousand a week or in round numbers 150,000 a year. We understand that the conspiracy has been running about that time."

"Nearly nineteen thousand pounds worth of spurious money in circulation!" Cullimore shook his head. "It's bad, but it might be worse."

"And nearly twelve thousand pounds a year netted," Sir Mortimer added. "Quite a profitable little enterprise, particularly if the profits had only to be

210

divided among three. What will your department do about it, Mr Cullimore?"

Cullimore glanced at him keenly.

"That really is rather a problem, Sir Mortimer," he admitted. "To all intents and purposes the money is good. Moreover, to recall it would be a virtual impossibility. At present I may as well admit that I do not see that we can do anything but accept it as genuine and let it continue to circulate. Of course, I am speaking off-hand and without proper consideration. But that is my present view."

For some time they continued discussing the matter and then Cullimore remarked: "The thing I cannot get over is the extraordinary skill with which the coins were turned out. This gang must surely have some technical training and it's not a trade that many men follow. You know nothing, of course, as to their identity?"

Sir Mortimer shook his head.

"We have their descriptions, though up to the present it hasn't helped us much. But I appreciate your point about technical training and we shall certainly make inquiries on these lines."

"Just the sort of thing one would expect from Jim Sibley. What do you say, Mr Cullimore?" said a new voice, and French looked with a sort of surprised interest at Dove, who had not yet spoken.

"'Pon my soul, I shouldn't be at all surprised to hear he had something to do with it," Cullimore returned. "He's the only man I know who could do such work. You haven't come across a stout, red-haired man in your inquiries, I suppose, Sir Mortimer?"

"Not so far. Who might Jim Sibley be, if it is not indiscreet to ask?"

"Up till three years ago he was an engineer employed at the Mint. He was with us for about seven years and I don't mind saying that, present company excepted, he was the most brilliantly clever man it has ever been my good fortune to meet. There was nothing about coining he didn't know and nothing he couldn't do with his hands. Extraordinarily resourceful too. It was a pleasure to see him tackle a difficulty, especially one which required some ingenious adaption of some tool or machine for its solution. As Mr Dove says, this coining business certainly suggests his hand."

"Why did he leave you, Mr Cullimore?"

The little man shrugged his shoulders.

"Rejected coins were disappearing. We were satisfied that he was stealing them, but we couldn't prove it. We asked him to leave."

"And did the thefts go on?"

"No, when he left there was no further trouble. There was not the slightest doubt of his guilt, but he was clever enough to prevent us getting proof."

Sir Mortimer not commenting, French asked if Mr Cullimore would kindly explain what rejected coins were and what was the object of stealing them.

"By rejected coins I mean those which are complete, but which fail to pass some of the tests imposed. For instance, a half-crown, otherwise perfect, might not ring quite true. It would therefore be rejected and would go back to the furnace to be remelted. Its value

212

to the thief, who would presumably put it into circulation, would be just two and sixpence."

"That seems a useful hint about this Sibley, sir," French said to the assistant commissioner. "With your permission I should like to ask these gentlemen for further particulars about him."

"By all means, French. Get what you can out of them while you have the chance."

But neither of the visitors could give information which seemed likely to lead to Sibley's apprehension. It was arranged, therefore, that French should send a man to the Mint to look up records and learn what he could from other members of the staff.

"I would go myself, sir," French went on, "but I don't want to leave the Yard for the present. I want to be here if any news of that girl should come in."

"Quite." Sir Mortimer turned to the others. "Inspector French is much upset as to the possible fate of one of the four girls who were changing coins for these ruffians. After worm — shall I say 'obtaining her confidence,' French? — she has disappeared and there is evidence that she has been kidnapped. Three of her predecessors were kidnapped and, I regret to say, murdered, almost certainly under similar circumstances."

"When I asked her for her confidence I promised her protection," French explained in a low tone.

"You mustn't blame yourself," Sir Mortimer declared. "I appreciate your feelings, but you mustn't let sentiment run away with you. You acted for the best and no one is omniscient."

"Thank you, sir. But you see why I want to stay at the Yard?"

"Yes, I approve of that. Well, gentlemen," he went on to the others, who had risen, "we are much obliged for your call and information. You may rest assured that we shall keep you posted in the developments of the case, and I trust you will advise us if further information comes to your knowledge."

"You may depend on us."

"Our friends are annoyed that we should have found out about this fraud before they did," Sir Mortimer remarked when the visitors had gone. "It evidently hurts their pride. Now, French, tell me exactly what you're doing. You can have all the resources you want. I quite agree that you must save that girl's life if it is humanly possible."

French detailed his plans.

"Is there anything else, sir, that you think I should do?" he asked.

"No, I think you have pretty well covered the ground. Carry on as you're doing and let me know directly anything comes in."

But nothing did come in. Every hour that passed made the affair seem more and more hopeless, while French grew more and more worried and despondent. That night he scarcely closed an eye, lying with the telephone beside him and hoping against hope to hear its bell summoning him to the Yard to follow up some clue which had just been reported. But though he had been disturbed on many a night when he was tired and would have given a good deal to remain in bed, on this occasion there was no call.

Next day at the Yard there was the same blank silence. He fretted and fumed through its insufferable hours until at last he told himself that he must give up hope, and began to fear that the only news he could expect would be that of the finding of the unhappy girl's body. And then late in the evening his weariness and lassitude changed to fierce energy and excitement. News had come in!

CHAPTER
SIXTEEN

In the Net

French's conversation with Molly Moran had given that young lady very seriously to think. From the beginning she had realised that the undertaking in which she was assisting was unlawful, if not actually criminal. She was not making a bid for French's sympathy when she told him that, since she had become involved, she had been miserable and in terror. This was the literal truth. Continually she had felt as if she were living on the edge of a volcano which might break out and overwhelm her at any moment. Visions of dismissal, of imprisonment, of ruin were constantly before her, and in spite of the money she was earning, she would have been thankful if she could have given up the whole thing and removed its evil shadow from her life.

But never in her wildest imaginings had she conceived that the affair could be weighted with murder or she herself in actual physical danger. The story of Thurza Darke and her two predecessors had therefore come to her as an appalling shock. Indeed, she realised that had it come alone she might easily have been driven by panic to take some step which might have precipitated the very crisis she feared.

216

Fortunately it had not come alone. The same conversation had brought her a feeling of overwhelming relief. She had confided her position to Scotland Yard. She had made a clean breast of everything. And she had not been arrested nor made to suffer any unpleasantness whatever. On the contrary she had been met with a sympathetic understanding such as she could not have expected from a police officer. She had been promised escape from the toils in which she had been caught as well as protection against her captors. In spite of the dark suggestion of murder, as she returned from the manager's room to her box office she felt happier than she had done for months.

During the remainder of that day it must be confessed that her thoughts were far from her job. Mechanically she counted change and shot out disc tickets while she speculated as to the developments which would take place as a result of her statement to French. Would Westinghouse, Style and Gwen Lestrange be arrested? If so, would she be a witness at their trial? She had always heard that giving evidence was a distressing ordeal, especially if one were cross-examined, as she would be by the lawyers for the defence. However, she was sure that French would see her through.

Excitement kept her awake for a good part of that night and next morning she came down with her mind keyed up to a high pitch of expectancy. What would the day bring forth? Surely with the knowledge the police now had some decisive step would be taken before night.

After breakfast she found herself with three hours on her hands before she must present herself at the cinema. Too restless to settle down at her boarding house, she determined to go for a walk in the parks, in the hope that the exercise might calm her mind. She was bursting to confide her story to all and sundry, but French's warning, as well as her own fears, deprived her of this relief.

As she walked, that other warning which French had given her seemed to stand out in her mind with an evergrowing insistence. Those addresses, the two places to which she must not go! The farther she walked, the more powerfully they drew her thoughts. That at Harrow did not so greatly interest her; it was far away. But Waterloo was near. She had been there scores of times. Not indeed in York Road, but close by. She would have liked . . . But of course she couldn't dream of going there after what Mr French had said.

She turned resolutely into the Green Park, but ever her thoughts reverted to the coachbuilder's yard. Presently without conscious volition on her part she found herself leaving the Park and walking in the direction of the river. "This will never do," she thought; then she saw that it could not possibly be any harm for her just to walk past the end of the street and look down. She had an uneasy twinge of conscience as she crossed Westminster Bridge, but the place drew her with extraordinary insistence.

Ten minutes later she found herself actually turning into Tate's Lane. But here she drew the line. French had said she was not to go and she would not.

Therefore contenting herself with a long, eager look down the unattractive thoroughfare, she put temptation behind her and passed on.

But still the place drew her. Aimlessly strolling on with time to kill, she thought she would go down the next parallel street and have a look at Tate's Lane from the other end. Perhaps from there she would see the builder's yard.

Thus it came to pass that at just five-and-twenty minutes past ten she was slowly sauntering along Killowen Street.

She had walked a hundred yards or more when she saw coming towards her a green saloon car with a figure which looked familiar at the wheel. No, she was not mistaken; it was indeed Mr Style! He was alone, and though he evidently did not see her, he was stopping, for he was slowing down and signalling to following drivers. As she stared at him, he turned the car into an entry almost beside where she was standing.

Her heart beat fast. Here was news for Mr French! Was it possible that where the tremendous organisation of Scotland Yard had failed, she was going to succeed? Mr French would revise his estimate of her. She would prove herself less of a fool than he had supposed.

At this moment, as he was crossing the footpath, Style saw her. For the fraction of a second an ugly gleam shone in his eyes, then he smiled pleasantly.

"Good morning, Miss Moran," he called. "This is an unexpected pleasure. What are you doing in this part of the world?" His tone was genial and he looked as if delighted by the meeting.

Molly felt a sudden urge to take to her heels. Then she saw that she could not do so. Style must not be allowed to think that she suspected him. She must satisfy him that the meeting was accidental and that she did not connect him with the half-crown affair, then pass on and ring up French from the first shop she came to. If she played her part well Style would suspect nothing and might stay where he was until French arrived. She therefore smiled back at him and walked up to the car.

"Good morning, Mr Style. I didn't expect to see you either, though I have often wanted to do so since our last meeting."

This piece of mendacity was due to a sudden idea. If she could engage Style in conversation she would probably be able to dispel any suspicion he might have formed. She would tell him that, having come into some money, she wished to resume betting on the Monte Carlo tables.

"In that case, I'm very pleased that you have found me. Will you excuse me for one second till I get the car out of the way of the traffic and then I shall be at your service."

He drove the car through the entry, turned it in the yard, and driving back, stopped inside the entry. Then he came out to Molly.

"Will you come into the office?" he invited. "Though I carry on bookmaking as a spare-time job, I do my real work in this shop. I think only one clerk is in at the moment, so that we can talk without being disturbed."

In spite of herself, Molly hesitated. French's warning recurred to her with increasing urgency. Was not this the very thing he had cautioned her against? Then she told herself she must not be a coward. She could see through the glass door into the office. There was nothing terrifying about its appearance. She could also see the clerk. With him there and in broad daylight and practically in a crowded street nothing could possibly happen to her. Nevertheless it was with some trepidation that she followed Style in.

He led her through the opening in the counter, drew a chair forward near the roll top desk, and asked her to sit down.

"I'm frightfully sorry," he declared, "but there is a bit of business I must attend to before we have our chat. Do you mind if I leave you for a moment? The inscription on a football cup which we are making has been changed, and I want to stop them before they cut the lettering."

He went out through the door into the entry and she presently saw him pass the window at the back. After a short stare the clerk had resumed his occupation of transcribing entries into a book. His appearance comforted her strangely. It was impossible, she felt instinctively, that anyone as stupid looking as he could be a party to a plot. The sight through the window of the stream of passers-by and the sound of their feet on the pavement still further eased her mind. Reassured, she set herself with a growing and wholly delicious excitement to await Style's return.

She was not impressed by the appearance of the office. It was positively filthy. The floor looked as if it hadn't been swept for weeks and dust lay thick on the furniture and the calendars and pictures on the walls. Compared with the spick and span establishment at the cinema, with its typewriters, calculating machines, filing cabinets and busy air, this place seemed like a reversion to the conditions of a century earlier. Molly smiled as she contrasted this uncouth, almost imbecile looking youth, with his untidy clothes and his inkstained fingers, with the neatly dressed, efficient staff to which she was accustomed.

Presently there came the whistle of a speaking tube. The youth put down his pen and slowly shuffled across the room to just behind where Molly was sitting.

"Yeh," he said. "Yeh. Two bob? Right."

He plugged the speaking tube, and taking his cap, lounged slowly out into the street.

Then Style re-entered. He in his turn went to the speaking-tube.

"Just a moment, Miss Moran, and I shall be at your service," he apologised as he picked it up. Then he began to speak. "Jenkins . . . Is that Jenkins? . . . Oh, Jenkins, I want you to get out that presentation shield that we did last month for Mr Hargreaves. I've sold it to Otway's people, and all we have to do is to change the inscription. You might —"

The voice suddenly trailed away into silence, as a sickening blow crashed down on Molly's head. She gasped, while momentary stars flashed before her eyes, then great waves of darkness seemed to rise up round her and she felt herself sinking down, down, down, into the blackness of unconsciousness.

Aeons of time passed, and then slowly sensation began to return to Molly Moran. First she realised only pain, indefinite but terrible pain. Then this seemed to localise in her head and to pass from there down through her whole body. Still she was in darkness, still a roaring sounded in her ears, but gradually she became conscious of movement. The place that she was in was shaking. At first she realised it only as something which added to her misery, but as she slowly regained her senses she realised where she was.

The sounds and the movement told her that she was in a motor car, travelling at a fair rate of speed. She was lying on the floor of the tonneau, entirely covered with a rug. This intelligence having sunk into her brain, experiment told the rest. Attempted movement showed her that her wrists and ankles were bound together and at the same time she found that she was securely gagged. Recollection of the scene in the silversmiths' office then returned to her and she knew what had happened. She had been kidnapped by Style!

Cold terror took possession of her as she remembered the story French had told her of the fate of the three girls who had attempted to betray the gang to the police. Had Thurza Darke, she wondered, lain bound in the tonneau of this terrible car as it jolted her on towards her doom? And what had befallen her at the end of the journey? Was drowning painful? As Molly pictured what might have happened, a cold sweat of fear broke out on her. It was too ghastly even to think of. And yet before many hours, before many minutes perhaps . . . Almost she swooned away again as she lay trembling in sick horror, her mind numb and scarcely functioning.

But she was young and strong. Gradually the paralysing sharpness of the first shock passed. Whatever faults she had, cowardice was not one of them, and soon she was striving desperately to pull herself together and to put as brave a face on the situation as she could. Things in her case were not quite so hopeless as in that of poor Thurza Darke. French was looking after her and she would immediately be missed. He would trace her to the silversmiths' and so learn what had happened. With the great organisation of the Yard behind him it could not be long until he found her. In fact he had evidently foreseen what might occur when he gave her his warning. Oh, that she had taken that warning!

But suppose he didn't trace her in time? She shivered, though she strove resolutely to shut her mind to the suggestion. She was not dead yet. While there was life there was hope.

To divert her mind from these harrowing thoughts, she fixed her attention more deliberately on her surroundings. Could she learn anything as to her destination from the sounds she heard?

It was immediately clear to her that they were bowling along at a fair speed on an extremely good road, asphalted, she thought. But she was conscious also of a reduction in the sound. She wondered if this were due to meeting fewer vehicles, as if so, it would indicate that they were getting farther from London. As she was considering the point they slowed down, and turning, she believed to the right, passed at a slower speed over a road with a much worse surface. After a few minutes they stopped altogether and she heard movements as if her driver were performing some gymnastic feat in the front seat. Then he got out and walked round the car and she heard a sort of click behind it. A moment later he re-entered and again they drove off.

For what she judged at about ten minutes, they drove off slowly along the bad road, then a slack, a sounding of the horn, another turn and they were once more on the smooth surface of a main thoroughfare. A few minutes of this, a few minutes of another byroad, and after another slack and turn, the wheels grated on the gravel of a drive. It was evidently a short one, then they bumped over some kind of obstruction and came to rest on a smooth surface. A rolling sound followed by a clang gave the necessary hint. They had driven into a yard and the big entrance gate had been shut behind them.

Presently she heard muffled voices and the door of the tonneau was opened. Then she felt herself being lifted and carried, still rolled in the rug, into some building and upstairs. One, two, three — six flights they went up. A few steps more on the level and she was laid down on something soft. Immediately the rug and gag were taken off and her bonds loosed.

She found herself in a dingy, whitewashed attic, with slanting ceilings and a skylight. The lower walls were stained and dirty and the boarded floor looked as if it had not been washed for a year. The furniture consisted of the bed on which she was lying, a chair, a table, a wash basin and a jug on an old box, a fireplace with fender and fire-irons but no fire, and in a corner a pile of old, untidy books. Over her were bending Style and Gwen Lestrange. They watched her in silence and at the look in their eyes a paralysing fear again swept over her.

"So you thought you could get off with it," Style said at last, and his voice was like the snarl of some vicious animal. "You thought you could play the traitor, speaking us fair and taking our money, and all the time spying on us and telling that cursed French what we were doing. You thought you could, did you?"

Molly was not prepared for this direct attack, but she countered as well as she could.

"What do you mean? I didn't tell anyone what you were doing. Sure, how could I when I didn't know myself?"

Style shook his clenched fist in her face.

"None of that, you traitor!" he answered harshly. "You've made the mistake of your life! You thought you had us, but we have you. You've betrayed us to French, but French can't help you now. You're in our power and you're going to pay."

Molly felt his gaze almost as a physical touch. It sapped her strength, but she clutched her courage with both hands.

"I don't know what you're meaning. Who is French anyway?"

226

"Liar!" Style shouted savagely. "Do you think we're fools? Do you think we act before we're sure? Let me tell you you've been watched. When you were telling French about us on the seat in Charing Cross Gardens yesterday, our agent was reading the paper within twenty feet of you! He saw you offering to show French your vanity bag and French's quick refusal. And we've watched you with him before. Fool!" he glared at her, "to think that you could fool us!"

To Molly, his abuse seemed to act as a stimulant. She felt her courage coming back.

"Ah," she retorted, "you're a bit off the track, Mr Style. That was me uncle you saw me with. He often meets me and takes me out."

Gwen Lestrange spoke for the first time.

"Little fool!" she said harshly. "Lies like that will only finish you up." But Style held up his hand.

"Just tell us his name," he demanded with a suddenly ingratiating manner and a sly look on his narrow face.

His friendliness terrified Molly even more than his anger. She realised that she had made a mistake and tried to recover.

"French," she admitted. "I see there's no good trying to deceive you. And he is an inspector at Scotland Yard. But he's me uncle for all that and he often takes me out and we've never discussed you or your affairs at all."

Style made a furious gesture.

"You —!" He used a foul name. "Do you know what happens to liars and traitors? Did you ever hear of Smith and the brides of the bath — how he drowned his wives in a bath? Well, that's what'll happen to you.

There's a bath in the next room all ready for you. The water rises slowly, slowly, slowly; up to your mouth, up to your nose, over your head. French won't help you then. Uncle indeed!" He paused and gazed gloatingly down at the helpless girl.

"He is me uncle," Molly persisted, but in spite of herself her voice faltered.

Again Style raved at her.

"Look here," he shouted. "You'll get one chance and one only. Tell us everything that passed between you and French and we'll let you go." He lowered his voice and spoke almost in persuasive tones. "Make a clean breast of the whole thing and we'll put you in the car and drive you to some deserted place from which you can make your way home. You'd like to be back in London, wouldn't you?"

He paused expectantly, but Molly did not answer.

"I'm sure you'd like to be free and home again. Well, tell us everything and you'll be there in a couple of hours. Hold back the least fact and you'll never see London again. No power in heaven or earth can save you. Tell me," he bent forward again and stared fixedly at her with his sinister eyes till she felt all the strength draining out of her, "tell me, did you ever hear of a young lady named Thurza Darke? Ah, I see you did. And none but French could have told you. You fool, to give that away! Well," his look became indescribably evil, "Thurza Darke wouldn't tell either, and she went and lay in the bath while the water slowly rose . . . We had to stop her screams lest they should be heard outside the house. Then after a long time the water rose

228

above her mouth and she didn't scream anymore . . . That's what'll happen to you. It's just next door." He motioned with his hand.

Molly couldn't speak. She felt too sick with horror. She lay gazing up at that narrow face with its evil, staring eyes and its expression of almost maniac hate. Presently Style went on:

"Perhaps you don't believe me? I tell you there were more than Thurza Darke. You never heard of Eileen Tucker, did you? Nor of Agatha Frinton? You don't know what happened to them? Well, you soon will." He pushed forward his face till Molly could scarcely refrain from screaming. "They went to the bath, and afterwards their bodies were found in rivers and quarryholes. But yours won't be found. We're going to hide it so that it'll never be seen again. No one will ever know what happened to you. Not even your beloved French will ever know, you —"

"Oh, for heaven's sake dry up and leave the girl till we're ready for her," burst in Gwen impatiently. "You've something else to do than stand here spouting like a bum actor in a dime circus! What about those machines?"

There was hatred in the look Style turned on Gwen and something of fear also. But his manner changed at once.

"You're right. We must get on," he said sullenly, then he turned again to Molly.

"There's a bell beside the fireplace. If you want to go back to town, ring and we'll come to hear your statement. If not — there's the bath in the next room!"

He walked to the door, let himself and Gwen out and locked it. Molly heard their steps descending the stairs, then all was still.

CHAPTER
SEVENTEEN

The Shadows Loom Nearer

For a few minutes after she had been left alone, Molly lay motionless, too full of horror even to think. She felt herself near death, and with all the intensity of her being she longed to live. Never had life seemed so sweet. She wanted to get out of this awful room, to see the sun, the fields, the trees, to feel the fresh air blowing on her cheek, to hear the birds and the sounds of life around her. More than that, she wanted to see her friends and to be once again amid her familiar surroundings in London. Even to be back in her box office, weary of it though she often had been, would now be heaven! But death was before her and at the very idea she grew once more sick and faint.

However, in the course of time her youth and health once again reasserted themselves. Things perhaps were not so bad after all. For the time being, at all events, she had a respite. It was evident that Style and Gwen were profoundly anxious to find out how much French knew. She believed they were going to keep her alive in the hope that they could make her tell. If so, she had only to refuse to speak and her life would be prolonged.

But this mood of optimism soon passed and terrible forebodings once more filled her mind. Was she safe under any circumstances? When they got all they wanted out of her, would her fate not still be that of Thurza Darke. For she did not believe their promise to free her if she did their bidding. They had not liberated Thurza Darke or her two unfortunate predecessors. These girls had almost certainly been forced to reveal what they knew, but it hadn't saved them.

The more she thought over her position, the lower sank her heart. There was just one ray of hope. She would be missed immediately. When she didn't turn up at the cinema they would 'phone to her boarding house. And her landlady would certainly ring up the Yard. Mr French would know within an hour or at most two. Then he would begin without delay to trace her. In fact, he was probably doing it at that moment. She had only to hold out so as to give him time. That was it. To hold out. She steeled her mind to the idea. No matter what happened, at no matter what cost to herself, she must hold out.

But would he trace her in time? She shivered as the thought forced itself into her mind. Then resolutely she pulled herself together. She must not allow herself to dwell on such a possibility.

To occupy her thoughts she got up from the bed and began to investigate her surroundings. The room was certainly very dilapidated. From the ceiling and walls hung festoons of cobweb and dust and scraps of old rubbish lay thick on the floor. The chair and table were of the plainest kind and the table rocked on three legs.

There was no water in the jug, and both it and the basin were thickly covered with dust. The truckle bed bore blankets but no sheets, and one of its legs was broken and tied together with string. In the otherwise empty grate was an accumulation of dirty rubbish. The skylight was out of reach, and there being no other window, she was unable to look out.

The pile of old books in the corner seemed to offer more promise of distraction and on these she tried desperately to fix her attention. All were dusty, but she turned them over in the hope of finding something which she might force herself to read. They were an extraordinary collection, all very old and all well thumbed. There were two Bibles, a large one with pictures, and a small thin one on India paper. There were *The Lamplighter*, *Queechy*, *The Fairchild Family*, *The Scarlet Letter*, and others, many of whose names she had never heard. Most of them were without inscription, but in one was written in a thin angular hand, "Christina Wyatt. February, 1864." Dully Molly wondered who Christina could have been and how her *Pilgrim's Progress* had survived during the sixty odd years since she had obtained it.

Among the collection was one book which might throw light on these problems and Molly, desperately anxious to fill her mind with something other than her own condition, picked it up and forced herself to read. It was an old manuscript book, bearing on the flyleaf the same name and containing notes in the same thin handwriting as well as pasted-in cuttings of various kinds. The book was of fair size, probably nine inches by six and an inch thick. Only about quarter of it had been filled, the remaining pages being blank. The notes took the form of a diary interspersed with moralisings, after the fashion of the period.

But Molly found it utterly impossible to fix her attention on it. Her own position was too precarious to allow her to think of anything else. Throwing the manuscript book back into the corner she sat down on the bed, buried her head in her hands and gave herself up to a detailed consideration of the situation.

She was trapped. Could she do anything to help herself? That was the burden of her thoughts. The problem had been in her mind subconsciously since her capture, but now she set herself definitely to think of ways of escape.

But the more she thought, the less hopeful the idea seemed. There was first of all the door. She got up and examined it. Opening inwards, it was strongly made and fitted with a mortice lock whose heavy bolt she could see passing across the narrow slit between the edge and the jamb. In no way could she force the door.

The chimney she could see at a glance was impossible. Even if she could have climbed it, the opening above the fireplace was too small to allow her to pass.

There being no windows, there remained only the skylight. Could she get out through the skylight?

She lay back on the bed, gazing up at the cobweb-covered square and calculating her chances. If she moved the bed beneath it, put the old box supplied as a washstand on the bed and put the chair on the box, she might be able to reach high enough. Suddenly eager, she sat up, listening intently. Not a sound reached her from the house. She decided to try the experiment at once. Her head still throbbed from the effects of the blow and she would rather have lain still. But the faint hope which had been aroused nerved her to effort.

Moving quietly and making as little noise as possible, she pulled the bed to the necessary position and built her tower. A moment later she was looking through the glass.

There was nothing much within view. A vast area of sky and the tops of a row of distant trees alone were visible. And when she tried to push up the skylight a further disappointment awaited her. It was fastened. Through one of the holes in the handle a screw had been passed. She tried to move the screw, but it was too firmly fixed.

For a moment she thought of breaking the glass, but she saw immediately that the metal bars of the frame were too close for her to squeeze between them. Baffled, she got down and stood thinking.

There seemed to be nothing that she could do. Slowly she took down the chair and the table and pushed the bed back to its place. She lay down, her thoughts approaching more nearly to despair than at any time since her capture. Oh, how she wished she had minded French's warning! What a fool she had been to imagine that she could stand up against members of a gang of this kind! What reason had she to imagine she was abler or cleverer than Thurza Darke? Oh, if when she saw Style she had just passed on with a bow and smile! If only she had done that she might now be sitting in her pay box at the Panopticon! She had been bored to tears with that box times without number, but now how she longed for it! She would have given all she possessed to be once more within its familiar walls. But no wishing would get her there.

Slowly the interminable hours dragged away, while the square of sunshine from the skylight crept across the wall, narrowed to a line and disappeared. Presently she realised that she was hungry. She had had no lunch and now it was after five o'clock. Surely they couldn't mean to starve her?

While she was considering the idea she dropped into a light sleep. She was roused by the rattling of the key in the door and sat up blinking as Style entered with a tray on which was set out a plain but sufficient supper.

"Asleep?" he said in some surprise. "It's well for you that you can take your position so easily! Or is it that you have not realised its seriousness?" He paused, then stepping nearer, spoke in a low, eager tone.

"Look here, you little fool. Once again I offer you your life and your freedom in exchange for your information. Tell me fully and without reserve of all your dealings with French and I'll let you go. You'll be taken in the car to a deserted place in the country and left to walk to the nearest station. Come on now; don't lose your last chance."

Molly, nerving herself to resist, did not reply. Style put down the tray and spoke with extreme earnestness. "For heaven's sake, Molly Moran, don't be such a fool!

Thurza Darke got this chance and didn't take it. She's dead now. Don't think I'm bluffing when I assure you that you'll die too if you don't do what I want. I offer you the choice of that or of freedom. Don't be such a darned fool!"

For a moment, Molly was tempted to tell of her interviews with French. Then something in his face, a look in his eyes, assured her that she was being deceived. There was no mercy there. He would never let her go. Her only hope was French. The thought of French cheered her and she rallied her courage.

"It's your fate that is sealed," she declared confidently. "Mr French knows all about you. You've been warning me, now I'll warn you. If anything happens to me, you'll hang! That's the way things are, Mr Style. Mr French knows all about Thurza Darke and he's taken precautions to prevent you repeating that. There's my warning to you."

Brave words, and yet Molly had scarcely spoken them before she felt sick with terror. It was a ghastly mistake to have said that about Thurza Darke! If Style believed it, it would remove her, Molly's, chief safeguard. If this gang thought the murder of Thurza could be brought home to them it would not save them to spare Molly. The penalty was the same for one murder as for two.

But this point of view did not seem to strike Style. He shook his head.

"Very well, fool," he snarled. "If you want to commit suicide, you can," and turning on his heel, he strode out, slamming and locking the door.

In spite of her almost frantic state of mind Molly felt a good deal better when she had finished the plate of cold roast beef and the bottle of cider which she found on the tray. If she could but get news of her whereabouts through to French she would be almost happy. Oh, to know that he was on the way to her help! Was there *nothing* that she could do?

Once again she lay down on the bed while she racked her brains over the problem. Was there *nothing* that she could do?

For an hour and more she tossed, then once again she heard footsteps and the door was unlocked. This time it was Gwen Lestrange. She carried a pair of sheets, a can of hot water, soap and other toilet requisites.

"Here you are, you little fool," she said contemptuously as she dumped her burden on the floor. "You don't deserve these, but we are not so bad as you imagine. But I warn you that unless you do as we want, you'll not need them by tomorrow night."

She did not wait for a reply, but went out quickly, locking the door after her.

Though Gwen's manner was so ungracious, the articles she had brought made a deal of difference to Molly. After a wash and brush-up she felt so much happier that when a little later she spread the sheets on her bed and turned in, she found herself actually comfortable. Then her anxiety and fatigues brought their own recompense and she slept dreamlessly. Indeed, when she woke it was broad daylight.

238

About eight o'clock Gwen brought her some breakfast and then began another weary and interminable day. She would not have believed how slowly time could pass. Hour after hour she lay on her bed, racking her brains over the problem of escape. Tales she had read of imprisoned heroines recurred to her, but in all of them some valiant young man had invariably appeared in the nick of time and had carried out the rescue. But in her case there was no such hero. She had herself to depend on and no one else in the world.

Except French. Again and again she pictured French following along that endless road from London. Momentarily she expected to hear of his arrival. But still the interminable silence remained unbroken.

Suddenly an idea flashed into her mind and she lay still, wondering whether there could be anything in it. The more she thought, the less sanguine she grew. However, it was better than nothing. A forlorn hope, but still a hope.

Again eagerly listening, she once more built her tower on the bed. Once more she climbed to the skylight. From her pocket she produced a penny. Could she turn the screw with it?

Alas, no! The edge was too wide to enter the slot. One encouraging fact however, she noticed which she had missed before. The wood round the screw was decayed. If only she could get something to fit the slot she felt sure the screw would not be hard to turn.

Twenty minutes wrestling with the problem brought her another gleam of hope. Going to the fireplace, she knelt down and began rubbing the edge of the penny on the hearthstone. And then hope changed once more to eagerness. The penny was deeply scratched. With perseverance she was sure she could rub its edge thin enough.

But she had not counted on the labour involved. She rubbed till her whole body ached before she succeeded. And then it was only to find that owing to the curve in the penny's edge it rose out of the slot when she tried to turn it.

This problem, however, was easier. Another exhausting period of rubbing on the hearthstone and she had ground a flat place on the disc, long enough to meet her purpose.

Few would blame her that she shed a few tears when, after all her weary work, she found she was still no nearer her goal. She could not turn the penny. But once more she pulled herself together. She had gone so far she *would not* be beaten. And very little further thought gave her the solution.

While she was considering some better way of gripping her penny, her eyes fell on the tongs. They were old-fashioned with a hinge and flat meeting faces, not the more modern spring kind with claw ends. It was the work of a few seconds to grip the penny in the tongs and try again.

But even yet she was not through. She found she could not hold the tongs tightly enough to prevent them opening. But she *would not* be beaten. Looking round in desperation her eye fell on the broken leg of the bedstead. In a moment she was kneeling on the

240

floor unwinding the cord which held it in place. Another few seconds and the legs of the tongs were tightly tied on the penny and she was again trying the great experiment. Her joy may be imagined when this time her improvised screwdriver worked!

The screw removed, she eagerly raised the skylight and looked out. But at the sight which met her eyes, her tears once again overflowed. All her work was unavailing. She was no better off.

Away from her the smooth slates of the roof stretched in every direction, from the ridge above to the gutter beneath and to the capping of the eaves to right and left. From where she stood the roof seemed like a great sloping table-land suspended in mid-air. It had no visible connection with the earth, which appeared beyond the gutter far below and a long way off. She thought she must be at the back of the house for there was no road or drive in sight. She was looking down into fields, behind which was a wood, forming the horizon. No human being was in sight nor even a house. So far as she could see, she might be the only remaining human being in the world.

No chance of escaping that way. She could not stand on that slope. With a thrill of horror she imagined herself climbing out, letting go the skylight frame, slipping down the smooth slates to the gutter, gripping it frantically, missing it . . . She shuddered. No, there was no hope that way. Nor was there any use in her making signals of distress. No one was there to see them.

Bitterly disappointed, she stood staring out, watching lest by chance some wanderer might appear in the fields whose attention she might be able to attract. But no one came.

Presently it occurred to her that the time for the evening meal must be near. Useless as this open skylight seemed, it would be wiser to keep the knowledge of it to herself. She therefore closed the sash, put back the screw loosely, replaced the furniture, took her screwdriver to pieces and lay down on the bed.

Only just in time! She had scarcely settled down when Gwen appeared with the meal.

Then followed a perfectly interminable night. This time she had not the necessary physical fatigue to make her sleep and she tossed restlessly during the long, dark hours. But morning came at last and with it breakfast and the prospect of another endless day.

She wondered what the plans of the trio could be. Gwen's threat as to her end coming before the previous evening had not been fulfilled. Either their plans had miscarried or Gwen had been bluffing. Reassuring, for what it was worth. But they could not keep her alive and a prisoner indefinitely. They must, she imagined, be waiting for some development, though what form it might take she could not imagine.

Like a century, the day dragged out its weary course. Lunch came, then Gwen with water, then supper, and still no ray of light or hope appeared to the girl. Then just as she was preparing for another long night of wakeful tossing, she got a new idea.

It was far more in the nature of a forlorn hope than the last, still, she reminded herself, it was a hope. But if she were to carry out her plan she must lose no time. It would be dark in less than an hour.

Now breathlessly excited, she jumped from the bed, took Christina Wyatt's old manuscript book, and cutting the thread which bound it, carefully withdrew some of the unused sheets. The double pages were of fair size, some fifteen inches by nine. Now, could she remember how to fold them? Once down the middle, the long way; then two corners back to the middle fold; then . . . For a time she experimented until at last there lay before her a dart like those she had made in hundreds in her schooldays. Eagerly she stood up and threw it. It floated gently across the room.

Mass production was now the order of the day. There were thirty-seven clean double pages in the book and in a few minutes thirty-seven darts lay in a little pile on the bed. As she folded, Molly thought out the message they would bear, so that by the time they were ready she had decided on the wording. Taking her fountain pen, she wrote on the top of each: "Finder for God's sake 'phone Victoria 7000 that Molly Moran is in this big house. Her life is at stake."

By this time it was getting dusk. As quickly and silently as possible Molly rebuilt her tower beneath the skylight, withdrew the screw and opened the frame. Then taking up a bunch of darts, she began to launch them one by one.

There was a gentle wind blowing towards the left. This picked up the darts and carried them well away from the house, over towards the fields. They floated well, and though most of them disappeared from view below the line of the roof, she saw some actually strike the ground.

The thirty-seven disposed of, she stood looking out, hoping against hope that someone would appear and get her message. But though she waited till it was quite dark, no one came in sight. At last with a profound sigh she closed the skylight, put the furniture in its place and lay down once more.

The reaction from her previous excitement had now set in and her depression became greater than ever. The darts, she felt, were no good. No one would find them and if anyone did he would think the message some child's prank and take no notice. Or, and this was a disaster which she had not thought of before, Gwen or Style might find them. What would happen to her then? And all the time in the background was the feeling of sick dread and horror when she thought of the fate of Thurza Darke. In the daytime there had been the excitement of what was happening to keep her up. Now there was nothing. She learned the awful loneliness of fear.

Fortunately from sheer exhaustion she fell asleep quite soon. But it seemed to her that her eyes had scarcely closed when she was awakened by a knocking at her door.

"Get up quickly," came Gwen's voice. "We're moving on. You must be ready in ten minutes. Here is a lamp."

The door opened, a small electric lamp was pushed in and the door was relocked.

Molly looked at her watch. It was still early — only half past eleven. What was now afoot? Had her time come?

She had not fully undressed, and almost sick with terror, she put on the remainder of her things. But she had not much time to think. Before she was ready Gwen returned, accompanied by Style. In silence they seized her and before she realised what was happening, her wrists and ankles were rebound, the gag thrust into her mouth and a handkerchief tied over her eyes. She felt herself being lifted and carried down the six flights of stairs and along passages to what was evidently a door, for the night air blew on her face. Then she was placed on a seat, she imagined in the same car as before, the engine was started up and they moved off. After a few yards they stopped and she heard above the noise of the running engine the clang of a gate, someone got in and sat down beside her and they moved off.

CHAPTER
EIGHTEEN

When Greek Meets Greek

It was shortly after eleven o'clock on that same night that the news came to Inspector French. Fed up with the whole business and tired out, he was actually on his way upstairs when his telephone rang.

"News of Miss Moran, sir," came the voice of the sergeant on duty at the Yard. "Hold the line and I'll put you through." There was a pause and then another voice sounded.

"Is that Victoria 7000? If so, I have a message for you."

"That's right. Repeat your message, please."

"I'm speaking from near Guildford. Between eight and nine my little nipper was coming home through a field and he found some paper darts with this message written on each: 'Finder for God's sake 'phone Victoria 7000 that Molly Moran is in this big house. Her life at stake.' We took it for a joke, but I am ringing up on chance."

French wiped a film of sweat off his forehead.

"It's no joke, I can assure you. This is Scotland Yard and we know something of the affair. Tell me, please, who you are and where you're speaking from."

An expression of amazed concern came through, then the voice went on: "I am Mr Edward Boland, speaking from my house, Dehra Dun, Elmford. I — I hope it's all right?"

"I hope so," French returned grimly. "Tell me, where is the big house mentioned?"

"It's at the other end of the village; Mr Trevellian's, the novelist's."

"Now, Mr Boland, could you lend a hand at your end? It may save the girl's life. How far are you from the police station?"

"It's in the village, five minutes walk from here."

"Good. Will you take the darts there and hand them to whoever is on duty and tell him your story. Tell him that you have rung me up, Inspector French, C.I.D., and say that I shall be going down immediately. Can you manage that?"

"Of course, Inspector. I'll do it now."

Ten seconds after Boland had rung off, French was talking to the Yard.

"Get six men together at once, Deane, and two cars with petrol for a long run. I want to go to Guildford. I'll be with you by the time you're ready. And look sharp, for goodness' sake! It's more then urgent."

By a lucky chance French picked up a taxi almost at his own door, and soon he was giving his instructions to Deane in person.

"Got those cars? Right. I want you to ring up the police station at Elmford, near Guildford. Tell them to take the message Mr Boland is bringing them seriously; they'll understand. Tell them that I'll be with them in an hour and that in the meantime they are to surround Mr Trevellian's house and allow no one to leave; let them detain on suspicion anyone who tries to. Explain that we think these people have a girl in their power and say that if the sergeant has any reason to suspect foul play he's not to wait for authority, but to break in. I'll stand the racket."

A minute later two fast cars left the Yard. In the first were French, Carter and two other men. The second contained Sergeant Harvey and another two assistants. Contrary to custom all were armed. French had with him the warrants he had previously obtained for the arrest of the members of the gang and he was determined, if necessary, to strain a point and use these to cover the search of the house.

"Don't kill anybody," he told the driver, "but don't be longer in one place than you need," and they roared on, their speed increasing continually as they left London farther behind.

The night was calm but dark. The light which should have come from the quarter moon was obscured by clouds. It was now fine, but there had been a shower earlier and the roads were heavy. Five-and-twenty minutes after leaving the Yard they ran through Kingston and in another twenty Ripley was left behind. From Ripley to Guildford they had a clear road and they fairly hummed along, but they had an exasperating slack through the town. Then for the remaining three miles they were able to put on another spurt, reaching the police station at Elmford just an hour and three minutes after starting. A constable hurried out and saluted.

"Inspector French, sir?" he said. "The sergeant's at Mr Trevellian's. First turn to the left and first house on the left-hand side." He pointed down the street.

A couple of minutes brought them to the place. As they drew up at the entrance to the drive two shadows moved forward.

"Inspector French, sir?" said the larger of the two. "I'm Sergeant Biggle and this is Mr Boland. No one has entered or left the house since we got your 'phone, but one of our men saw a car leave as he was on his rounds."

"At what hour was that?"

"Eleven-forty, sir. It was too dark to see details, but he believed it was Mr Trevellian's green Armstrong-Siddeley. They turned in the direction of Farnham."

"Could he say how many people were in it?"

"No, it is a saloon and it was too dark to see more than the outline."

French nodded. "Now as to Mr Trevellian. Describe him, please."

"A rather stout, undersized man with bright red hair, a pale complexion and blue eyes."

French felt a sudden thrill. This could surely be none other than that Jim Sibley of whom Cullimore and Dove had spoken, the engineer who had been dismissed from the Mint for theft.

"Anyone else live here?"

"Mrs Trevellian. She's a tall, well-built woman with fair hair and complexion, blue eyes and a strong chin."

Better and better! Gwen Lestrange, for a certainty!

"Right. They're the people we want. Anyone else?"

"There's. Mr Marwood, Mr Elmer Marwood. He's brother to Mrs Trevellian, and lives with them. He goes into town every day, mostly in Mr Trevellian's car. A thinnish, pale-complexioned man with a small straw-coloured moustache and glasses. That's all."

Style! That made four, including Welland. French would have betted long odds it was the lot. He turned to Carter.

"Take charge, Carter," he directed. "Surround the house and go in and search it. If they don't open immediately, break in. You needn't mind making a noise. Only look sharp. Now, Mr Boland, you told me your son found these darts between eight and nine, but you didn't ring up till after eleven. I'm not finding fault, sir, but could you not have done better than that?"

"Awfully sorry, Inspector, but you see I didn't know about it. My wife and I were dining out and the servant was on leave. The boy was alone in the house. He's only eight. Against orders he waited up for me, and though I thought it was a hoax, I rang you up at once."

"I understand, sir. It was not your fault, but it was a pity all the same. Now, Sergeant," he went on to Biggle, "I want you to go back to your office and put through a general call to all surrounding stations. Describe the car and the party and give their direction as far as we know it. Where would you get to if you went through Farnham?"

"Southampton or Salisbury, I should think, sir."

250

"Southampton it'll be," said French. "They're making for the ships. Well, ring up, will you, especially to Southampton and places on the way there. Tell them to report to you if there is news, and stand by to repeat it to me when I ring up. That all clear?"

The sergeant repeated his instructions, and French hurried after Carter. In some way the latter had obtained entrance, for a constable stood guarding the open hall door. Within a rapid search was in progress.

"Got through the pantry window, sir," said Carter, appearing suddenly in the hall. "The house is deserted, but they've been coining in the cellar, though the machines are gone. Down there, if you'd like to have a look."

"I'll run down for a moment. Make sure that girl's not in the house and meet me in the hall."

French's "look," brief though it was, left him still more impressed with the amount of labour which had been put into the coining scheme. The cellar, a large, white-washed room, had been fitted up elaborately. The windows had been built up, but a system of Tobin's tubes had been installed for ventilation, and the place was brilliantly lit with electric light. On the benches lay hundreds of partially finished coins, bits of tools and other debris. The place where presses had stood were clearly marked, but all the machines had been removed. There had been several of these, some, the foundations suggested, of a considerable size.

The sight cleared up a point which had been bothering French, namely, why the gang had not made off more quickly after becoming suspicious that the police were on their track. The removal of these machines supplied the reason. These people were not going to give up coining because that particular pitch had grown too hot for them. Clearly they were going to break fresh ground and start again. In some other great city the mortality among box office girls would soon be on the up-grade — unless he, French, stopped it.

When he reached the hall Carter was descending the stairs. No, there was no trace of anyone in the house, but there was a partially furnished attic, the only room above the ground floor which showed signs of recent occupation, in which the young lady might have been imprisoned.

"And that," went on Carter, "is next the field where Mr Boland said the darts were found. I expect she was there all right."

"Very well; let's get on."

As none of French's party knew the roads, they took a local constable as guide. Warned of the urgency of the case, the driver put on every ounce of power and they snored on at a breakneck pace through the night. Fortunately the road was good and other traffic practically non-existent, or disaster might have overtaken them. French sat in front, tense and watchful, though with his mind full of the problems which still remained. He believed that this was the last lap and that the party in front represented the entire gang. He could now see the function of each. Trevellian, or Sibley, to make the stuff; Style to take it to town and to obtain and bring down the raw materials; Welland to see to its distribution; Gwen to trap the necessary girls and doubtless do other odds and ends as might be required. And Sibley's guise of an author was just what might have been expected. It would account for his living in the country as well as for his long absences during the day. French could imagine the casual caller. "Where is Mr Trevellian? I should like to ask him so and so." "Oh, he's writing. He doesn't like to be disturbed when he's at work." It was a good, well-thought-out scheme. These people had deserved to succeed.

Presently there came houses — Farnham.

A hurried call to Elmford told them that there was no news and the chase was resumed. French was now much more anxious. He was running on towards Southampton on the mere strength of his summing of the probabilities. But he might be wrong. That start towards Farnham might have been a blind, and every mile might easily be increasing his distance from the quarry. If so, Molly Moran's chances would be pretty thin — assuming, indeed, that she were still alive.

But there was nothing else for it, and they hurried on. French glanced at his watch; it was just past two o'clock. If the gang had gone this way, they must have passed nearly two hours earlier and nearly half an hour before he telephoned. If they had been seen it would only have been by the merest chance.

At five minutes past two they ran into Alton and stopped at the police station. Again no luck! The Elmford sergeant telephoned that he had heard nothing.

The difficulty of French's problem was now increased tenfold. Should he go on? If the others were not making for Southampton, to do so would probably mean losing them altogether. But there was no time for hesitation. Rightly or wrongly he would back his judgment.

"On towards Southampton," he ordered, and once again they began their mad rush through the endless night.

At twenty minutes to three they reached the suburbs of Winchester and a couple of minutes later French was again ringing up Elmford. Then his weight of fear and doubt was suddenly eased and he felt a thrill of the keenest satisfaction. There was news!

On receiving Sergeant Biggle's call, the officer in charge at Southampton had instantly sent round the roads in the vicinity to warn the patrols who were already out on their beats. Just five minutes earlier one of these men had returned to say that a car answering the description in question had passed through the village of Old Netley at about 2.00a.m. It had come from the direction of Hedge End and gone on towards the sea. Hedge End was in a direct line from Winchester to Netley.

"Netley! Hard as you like!" French cried as he swung himself back into the car.

Luckily their guide had once been stationed at Southampton and knew the district. They ran on at full speed to Botley, then turning back west, went south through Hedge End. There they left the main road and at a necessarily reduced speed ran through Old Netley and down to the shore of Southampton Water at the end of the little town of Netley.

Here was another problem for French. The road down which they had come debouched at right angles

254

into a road running parallel to the shore. Should they turn up or down channel?

"Where does that road go to?" he asked the guide, pointing down towards the sea.

"Just to Netley town and the hospital, sir, though you can get on to Hamble. But they wouldn't have gone that way because there's a direct road from Winchester to Hamble through Hound."

"Very well; turn to the right."

This, the guide explained, would bring them in a couple of miles to Southampton, through the suburb of Woolston. French, deciding that he would make for the police station, nodded.

After passing a grove of trees at Hilton the road ran down along the sea, being separated from the actual beach by a strip of unfenced grass, some thirty yards wide. To be so near a great port, the place was extraordinarily secluded. The clouds had now uncovered the quarter moon and so far as French could see in the dim light, there was not a house in sight. Away in front were the lights of Southampton and out on the water were the riding lights of steamers, with an occasional twinkle from the Hythe shore opposite. But the nearer shore was dark and deserted. Anything, thought French, might go on there and no one would be a bit the wiser.

As he looked out over the black water his face suddenly grew grim. He thought he could now account for the route the others had taken. They were going to Southampton all right, but they had something to do first. There was dangerous evidence — to be destroyed. There in the water, somewhere out in the darkness towards Hythe he dared swear was now floating the body of the poor little Irish girl. He sighed as he thought of the narrow chance on which the thing had turned. If only that man Boland had not been out when his son found the darts! Ah well, it couldn't be mended now. But there was still one thing to be seen to and French set his teeth as he thought of it. They should pay, these ruffians, pay in full measure, pressed down and running over. Until all four were either in gaol or dead, he would not rest. Poor little Molly!

And then something happened which completely altered his outlook and set him thinking furiously. The road turned sharply inland and as they swung round the bend they passed a man.

He was walking to meet them and owing to the curve he momentarily got the full benefit of their headlights. But that moment was enough. In spite of the fact that his hat was pulled down over his eyes and his collar turned up about his cheeks, French recognised him. It was Style!

French had never seen Style, but he had had so many descriptions of him that no doubt was possible. The man was walking quickly as if late for an appointment.

For five seconds French thought hard. Then as they passed round the curve out of Style's view he stopped the cars and hurriedly assembled his men.

"Style!" he explained rapidly. "After him, but on your lives not a sound!"

For big men, as most of the officers were, their movements were surprisingly silent as they followed French at the double. When they regained the shore the grass muffled their footsteps and such slight sounds as they made were lost in the dreary moaning of the wind and the plash of the waves on the beach. Presently they caught sight of Style. He had left the road and was picking his way down to the water's edge. French and his followers dropped on their hands and knees and crawled on till they were directly behind him.

Style, having reached the edge, stopped and stood looking out over the water. He seemed to be doing something with his hands, but French could not imagine what.

Then he knew. From the sea came three flashes as from an electric torch, and with these as a guide, French found he could detect a blacker smudge against the dark water. A vessel of some kind, close inshore and showing no lights.

As they watched, a second smaller smudge detached itself from the other. Someone was coming ashore.

Almost instinctively a plan flashed into French's mind. After a whispered word to his men he began slowly to creep up behind Style. Style seemed uneasy, but it was not till French was beside him that he turned. At the same instant French sprang and with a muffled cry the man came down.

He fought like a maniac, but Carter and Harvey had come up and he had no chance. In a few seconds he was helpless, bound and gagged.

"Once again," whispered French.

He had snatched off Style's hat and putting this on and turning up his collar, he stood waiting as the other had done. The boat was now close inshore and revealed itself as a collapsible punt with a capacity for two. A short, stout man was rowing.

"Thought you'd never be back," the stout man grumbled as the punt touched the ground. "For heaven's sake look alive now. We don't want to be here all night."

Further remark died off into a kind of gurgle. French had seized him by the throat. This man also after the first moment of surprise fought like a tiger, but once again the odds were too heavy. In a few seconds he lay bound beside his accomplice.

"Now, Carter, it's you and me for it," French panted. "However many there may be they're two fewer for this. You, Harvey, get the others and have those two men into one of the cars. Then come down and be prepared to lend a hand."

Rapidly they righted and emptied the boat, which had been upset in the struggle, and French and Carter got in.

"I'll row," French decided. "I'm more the size of that second fellow. You take Style's hat and turn up your collar. And have your gun ready."

Old hand as he was, French's heart was beating more rapidly than could be accounted for by his scrap as he pulled out towards the launch. These were desperate men, their escape almost consummated. They would not lose their freedom for the sake of the lives of a couple of policemen. French had no delusions as to the possibility that neither he nor Carter might ever see another sunrise.

"We want to take them alive," he said in low tones, "but if you see them going to shoot get in first."

The boat was closer inshore than French had supposed. As they came they saw that she was a motor launch of some forty-five feet long. She seemed a sea boat, well decked over forward. On her deck astern stood a man and woman.

"It's about time you thought of coming," called out the man when they were within earshot. "What the — hell were you monkeying about ashore? We'll not be clear of the Island by daylight at this rate."

Welland! And the woman was certainly Gwen Lestrange! French murmured a husky reply in a tone as like that of the former oarsman as he could. But his effort was not good enough. The two started and called out simultaneously in tones of urgent anxiety.

"Sibley!" cried Welland. "Speak clearly, can't you!" while Gwen shouted: "Jim. Is that you? Answer!"

French put down his head and pulled with all his might. The boat bounded forward. There was a sudden scuffle on deck. "Look out, it's French," came in a shrill scream from Gwen, while with a savage oath Welland roared: "Start the — engine! For your life, Gwen! I'll pot them if they try to come aboard!" The voices of both had an edge of desperate urgency.

Like a flash the girl leaped to the cabin door, and after fumbling at its lock, disappeared within. Welland at the same time dashed across the deck, seized what appeared to be a top coat and began hurriedly searching its pockets. At that moment the boat came alongside and both French and Carter sprang at the rail and began to climb aboard. But they were too late. Before French reached the deck Welland found what he wanted. His hand flew up and in it was something shining. And then, just as he was about to fire, a flying figure appeared from the cabin — the figure of a girl. She dashed to Welland and as the jet of flame spurted from the pistol, struck desperately at his arm. French felt a searing pain in his head, but he was not disabled and he sprang across the deck to Welland. He had a vision of the girl reeling wildly back, and with her scream ringing in his ears, he closed. For a moment it seemed as if things would go badly with him. Welland was the bigger man and he was evidently in excellent training. He got in a left-hander over French's heart which left the latter sick and quivering. But French concentrated his whole will-power on holding his grip of the other's wrist and preventing him turning the pistol inwards. Then Carter joined in and the thing was a matter of time. In three minutes Welland was bound like his confrères ashore.

"Look out for Gwen," gasped French as he dragged himself over to where Molly Moran lay in a motionless heap against the deckhouse wall.

Carter locked the cabin door, then turned to help with the unconscious girl. They stretched her out on the deck and bathed her face and hands.

"Only stunned, I think," French went on hoarsely. "I suppose you realise, Carter, that if she hadn't been such a plucked one, you and I would be down in Davy Jones' locker now. You owe your life to her, man, and so do I."

260

"I didn't see just what happened. It was all over and we were scrapping round before I knew where I was."

"It's clear enough what happened. They had locked her in the cabin and when Gwen went to start the engine she didn't wait to close the door. Molly dashed out and knocked up this beauty's hand as he was firing. It was a close thing, Carter. I felt a bullet pass my head. Ah, there. Thank God for that!"

Molly had opened her eyes and was making a pathetic attempt to smile. At sight of it, French forgot himself in the most lamentable manner. Fortunately, no one who mattered was there to see his lapse. French — alas that it must be recorded! — caught the girl up in his arms and implanted not one but two hearty kisses on her mouth.

"My word, Molly, but you're the goods!" he declared in rather shaky tones. "If I was about a hundred years younger, and there was no Mrs French, you'd be listening to a proposal of matrimony. You're really nothing the worse, child?"

And the abandoned creature, instead of indignantly protesting against his conduct and demanding a commission of inquiry into the whole circumstances, smiled up into his face and agreed that, everything considered, she was really very well indeed.

CHAPTER
NINETEEN

Conclusion

Little more remains to be told.

When Gwen Lestrange — to give her the name by which she had been known to French — she was really Mrs James Sibley — saw from the cabin the turn affairs had taken, she surrendered at discretion. It appeared that there were no other members of the gang, and before morning all four prisoners were safely lodged in the cells.

With the additional knowledge he now possessed, French immediately began a further inquiry into their misdeeds and before long the entire details of the coining scheme were revealed.

It seemed that Jim Sibley had long been convinced as to the possibility of profitably counterfeiting silver coins. Even with these composed of nearly pure silver, he believed the thing could be done, but the passing of the Act of 1920, reducing the proportion of pure silver to 50 per cent, and the subsequent fall in the price of silver, left no doubt whatever in his mind. When, therefore, he found himself dismissed from the Mint, it had occurred to him that an auspicious time had arrived to test the truth of his convictions.

He was up, however, against one overwhelming difficulty. He had no capital, and the inception of his scheme required what was to him quite a big sum. For a time his plans hung fire and then he saw his way.

From some of his dubious acquaintances, he had heard from time to time of a Mr Curtice Welland, or as he then called himself, Hervey Westinghouse. Welland, to give him the name he afterwards took, was looked upon by the fraternity of the underworld as an example of a strikingly successful career. He was reported to live by blackmail, and it was hinted that on different occasions he had paid large sums for "jobs," mostly the burglary of some well-known person's house for letters of a profitable type. Sibley came to the conclusion that if Welland could be interested in his scheme, the necessary capital would materialise. He introduced himself, sounded the other, and to make a long story short, the firm of Sibley, Sibley & Welland came into being.

When they came to work out the details they found that a fourth member would be required. Here again Welland filled the breach. In his toils was a man called Webster, afterwards "Style." Owing to an irregularity in connection with the signature of a cheque, Style had handed over his freedom to Welland and he was now told what he must do. Unwillingly Style came in and the quartet started work.

The necessary machines were ordered to be sent to certain ports in the names of various foreign medal making firms, to be kept till called for. There Style, in the guise of an emissary from the foreign firms, obtained them, ostensibly to arrange for their shipment. In reality he ran them in his car to the house near Guildford, which in the meantime had been rented by the Sibleys.

Some means of buying silver without arousing suspicion in the trade being an essential, the silversmiths' works were purchased, Style becoming the "manager." All the members of the staff who showed any intelligence were dispensed with, enough being retained merely to keep the place open. Style bought the silver in the name of Theobald & Grudgin and secretly transferred to his garage what Sibley required, bringing it home to Guildford in the car.

The guise of an author enabled Sibley to withdraw himself during long periods on each day, and his wife helped him with the manufacture of the coins. It was considered unsafe for either of these two or Style to take part in their distribution, so this was undertaken by Welland in the way French had already discovered.

Every morning and night, while passing along a quiet stretch of by road, Style changed the number of his car and slightly altered his appearance by putting in a different set of false teeth, brushing his hair and moustache differently and putting on glasses and a different shaped hat. Because of this, and also of the fact that in his earlier circular, French had described the grey car used by Welland instead of Style's green vehicle, he succeeded in avoiding recognition.

It was part of Style's duty to spend a good part of his time in shadowing the four box office girls whom they had made their dupes. French's inquiries were thus early known to the gang. Welland instantly saw through the trick of the broken window and this convinced the gang that they were in dangerous waters. The manufacture of coins was suspended, while Sibley and his wife, both disguised, shadowed the girls. French's interview with Molly in the Charing Cross Gardens thus became known to them and they saw that they were on the eve of discovery. At once a message was got through to Style to supply Welland with "good" coins for the girls. Style kept a supply in his safe for this purpose, and he passed good bundles to Welland, replacing them with the four faked lots he had brought to town. It was in this way that the coins obtained by French from Molly proved to be good, while those which he found in Style's safe were faked.

The eventuality which the quartet found themselves up against they had long foreseen and provided against. Their idea was that if England should get too hot to hold them, they would transfer their activities to France. Welland had therefore bought the launch, storing it at Ryde. They were determined, however, not to go without their plant, and preparations for the removal of this were in hand when the whole situation was altered by Molly's recognition of Style at the silversmiths'.

Style instantly recognised that if Molly were allowed to see French again they were done for. French would get on his trail and would find the house at Guildford before the plant had been got away. He therefore decided to kidnap her, so as to gain the necessary time for this operation.

The question of whether she should not be murdered like those of her predecessors who had shown a desire to communicate with Scotland Yard was carefully considered, and her life was spared as a sort of forlorn hope. If by some unlikely chance French should discover their flight before they got clear away, Molly was to be exhibited and French was to be told that if he attempted to prevent their escape she should be shot then and there in cold blood. They thought this might make him hesitate sufficiently to enable them to effect their purpose.

By the evening of the day on which Molly was kidnapped, all the preparations for the flight were complete, and if the gang had then bolted, in all probability they would have got clear away. But an unexpected hitch at the last minute delayed them for two days and led to their undoing. Welland found that he could not start the engine of the launch, and he lost two vital days at Ryde in getting the defect put right.

The working out of a method of transhipping their plant from car to launch proved one of their most difficult problems. The need for secrecy forbade the use of a wharf and crane and they knew of no natural harbour or rock from which the machines could be embarked. They therefore chose the position on Southampton Water, one of the rare "hards" on a shore of soft and sedgy flats. At low water they ran the car down on the beach, unloaded and buoyed the machines, and when the tide rose floated the launch to the place and hoisted the machines on board. Two journeys of the car had been necessary to transport all the plant, the second being that by which Molly had been taken. On reaching the shore for the second time, the balance of the machines had been unloaded, and the whole of the party except Style had gone on board. Style utilised the time until the tide rose high enough to lift the machines in attempting a further safeguard. With the object of confusing the chase, should one materialise, he had run the car into Southampton, and it was when walking back after abandoning it there that French and his party met him.

Though French found out all these details without much difficulty, he was at more of a loss to prove the responsibility of the gang for Thurza Darke's murder. But eventually he managed this also. The attendant at the Milan identified Gwen Lestrange as the young woman who had called for Thurza on the night of her disappearance, and Dr Lappin, of Lee-on-the-Solent, swore that Style exactly answered the description of the man who was attending to the engine of the grey car on the road near Hill Head. This evidence, added to the rest that French had collected, secured a verdict of guilty, and eventually all four paid for their crimes, Welland and Sibley on the scaffold and the other two with life sentences.

Before his death Welland made a full confession. In it he admitted that he and Sibley had murdered all three girls in the horrible and revolting way with which Style had threatened Molly. Following the example of Smith, the "brides in the bath" murderer, they had drowned their unfortunate victims in the bath in the house at

Guildford before disposing of their bodies in the quarry hole, the river and the sea respectively.

Of all the interested parties, Molly came off the best. Not only was she not prosecuted, but on the ground that the amount was unknown, the question of her ill-gotten gains was not raised. Most immorally, therefore, she found herself in possession of the nice little sum of nearly four hundred pounds as her share of the affair.

As for French, the consciousness of work well (if slowly) done was his reward. The case had been an unusually troublesome and disappointing one, but he had at least the satisfaction of knowing that he had not only in all probability saved Molly Moran's life and the lives of other girls who might have fallen into the hands of the gang, but had cleared out a nest of evildoers whose removal was essential to the welfare of the entire country.

Other titles published by Ulverscroft:

THE GROOTE PARK MURDER

Freeman Wills Crofts

When a signalman discovers a mutilated body inside a railway tunnel near Groote Park, it seems to be a straightforward case of a man struck by a passing train. But Inspector Vandam of the Middeldorp police isn't satisfied that Albert Smith's death was accidental, and he sets out to prove foul play in a baffling mystery which crosses continents from deepest South Africa to the wilds of northern Scotland, where an almost identical crime appears to have been perpetrated.

THE 12.30 FROM CROYDON

Freeman Wills Crofts

1930s, somewhere over the English Channel: a family from Yorkshire is on the 12.30 flight from Croydon to Paris — but by the time the plane lands, Andrew Crowther, a wealthy retired manufacturer, is already dead ... Flash back four weeks. Andrew's nephew, Charles Swinburn, is facing the prospect of bankruptcy. In desperation, he devises a cunning scheme to tempt a rich young woman into marriage and dispose of his uncle, thus solving all his financial problems. But all does not go according to plan, and Charles's bad luck is compounded when Inspector French shows up on the scene ...